Last
copy

2015

The Legacy

PETER TURNBULL

2042243115

First published in Great Britain in 2005 by
Allison & Busby Limited
Bon Marche Centre
241-251 Ferndale Road
London SW9 8BJ
http://www.allisonandbusby.com

A catalogue record for this book is available from
the British Library.

10 9 8 7 6 5 4 3 2 1

ISBN 0 7490 8313 1

Printed and bound in Wales by
Creative Print and Design, Ebbw Vale

9504

Chapter One

in which a murder is declared.

The man loved birdsong. Perhaps, more specifically, he loved the sound made by the British songbirds in woodland or a forest upon a summer's day. He was an educated man and was aware that any ornithologist would advise that the "songs" were in fact sounds of threat and warning given off by each bird in defence of its own personal space. That fact did not upset him, because to him, as to most human ears, the sounds were musical, enchanting, mystical. He always felt uplifted by the sound, it inspired him and each day – but particularly during the summer – he walked the woodland near his house receptive to the muse visiting him by means of the sounds of British songbirds in full throat. He walked on, following a distinct and baked-hard track through the woodland, which undulated interestingly. The tracks of bicycle tyres that had clearly been made when the soil was damp had, by then, been baked hard, and attested to the joy children had obtained by cycling along the path. The man could understand their joy, not only was the path as smooth as tarmac, it went up and down in a series of hollows and summits: great fun on a bicycle, especially if there were just three or four good pals in the gang – the wood to themselves – and blessedly free of any danger from road traffic. The man emerged from the wood and, leaving the canopy of the trees, was hit by the weighty glare of the mid-afternoon sun. He turned the peak of his baseball cap towards the sun and continued to follow the path as it drove across a silent meadow of knee-high grass, towards a second stand of trees, more shade and more lovely, lovely birdsong. He strolled on, enjoying the day, enjoying the lush foliage about him, eagerly anticipating the sound and the calming presence of the trickling brook that he knew ran through the stand of trees he was then approaching. He entered the shade of the second small wood as beads of sweat ran down his forehead. He heard the gurgling sound of sweet water, as he had expected, and he heard the melody of the songbirds, also as expected. There was, however, another sound, a sound he had heard before on many, many occasions as had most, if not all, adult human beings at some point in their lives. And like all that had heard the sound, he had come to associate it with something unpleasant to human taste: it was the loud buzzing sound of hundreds of flies. The man had walked the path on a near daily basis throughout all four seasons and had done so for many years. It was the first time he had heard such a sound at any point along the route of the path. He thought that that made the sound doubly surprising and doubly suspicious. The sound came from ahead and to the left of the man, where stood a thick area of gorse in an area surrounded by trees, a meadow within the second wood which had, over time, been colonised by gorse. The man walked from the path, weaving his way between the trees until he stood at the edge of the tree line. Before him was the swathe of gorse, three or four feet high in places, a sea of yellow flowers on the end of stems of vicious spikes, a species of plant that likes itself, bush upon bush nestling closely, sometimes covering areas as large as a football pitch, impenetrable to all but the smallest of creatures and so well protected but oh so vulnerable to fire, so inflammable. Any who has seen gorse burn will never forget the sight – the ferocity of the flames, the speed at which it tracks on hot, dry days and nights, as if the very plant secreted petroleum. The man had seen gorse burn twice in his life and had been terrified on both occasions – a small area of gorse on a slope, about the area of a car park in front of a small supermarket, with bushes no more than three feet in height had within seconds, less than half a minute, become an inferno with flames twenty or thirty feet high. It would not, thought the man as he witnessed it from a close but safe distance, be an exaggeration to call it a firestorm, the flames merging into one central column as air was sucked from the surrounding area. Any person trapped in the gorse could not have escaped. Mercifully, the fire burned out rapidly and the gorse did not recover until the next spring. From the moment he had first seen gorse burn, the man had been grateful for the spikes on the branches of the bush, any temptation to enter a stand of gorse was removed, keeping him safely outside. The second time he witnessed gorse burn was a less extensive fire, just a single bush on a cultivated area of land, but once more he found the amount of flames generated from a single, modest bush, awesome. The man had thus developed a healthy respect for gorse and was reluctant to force his way into such a large area of it. The thought of entangling his foot in a root just as another walker should carelessly discard a smouldering cigarette butt into the sea of yellow was too horrible to contemplate. Yet…yet, something was in the gorse, something that was not there the previous day at this time, and it was something that had attracted the bluebottles in their hundreds, if not thousands. The black cloud hovered over the bushes and it seemed to the man to be four feet deep below that until the bottom most insects were laying their larvae on whatever it was that had attracted them.

The man stood and pondered the cloud of flies.

It was sinister: that, he felt, was plain.

He considered phoning the police using his mobile phone to report – what? A cloud of flies? He thought he knew what reaction he would get. He considered setting the gorse alight, a controlled burning which, when it had died out and cooled, would allow him to enter the shrubs without incurring any risk to himself. Eventually, he realised the only thing he could do – the one thing he had to do – was to force himself into the gorse, negotiating the needle-like spikes as gingerly as he could, hope that the vegetation doesn't catch fire whilst he's in its midst, and if it did, accepting he'd have to run through it to the safety of the tree line no matter the discomfort, and trusting to luck that he didn't trap his foot in a root in the process.

He dropped his rucksack. He thought the cloud of flies was perhaps equivalent to the length of a bus away from him. If he moved carefully, finding the path of least resistance, he estimated it might take him ten minutes to reach it. He was to recount later that the exploit took him nearer a full half hour.

The body, for that was what the man discovered had attracted the flies, lay on its front. It was more than just a body, and in some ways, as he would recount later when "sharing" the experience with friends, it was also less than a body: it was more because it presented a sudden and completely unexpected image which the man would never be able to wholly drive from his mind's eye, and it was literally less than a body. It was without clothing, without hands and without a head.

The man waved angrily at the flies but their response was partial and very short-lived. Within seconds those few that had flown a little way away returned, so that in the gorse, chest down, was the headless and handless body of a naked man, covered with a carpet of flies and above that an excited cloud of flies, as if waiting their turn to lay larvae on the lovely, fresh flesh. The man turned and picked his way back through the gorse to the path, not seeming to feel the occasional prick of a gorse needle, reminding himself that you have to be alive to feel, whether discomfort or pleasure, you have to be alive and that gave him a distinct advantage over the other man. His life, he thought, as the gorse tore at his legs had had its ups and downs but he had never got so far down that he was a mutilated, naked corpse which had been abandoned to the flies. He was to recall little about the return journey through the gorse, save only that it seemed, and probably was, a great deal speedier than the outward one. With his legs stinging from multiple scratches he reached the path and knelt in front of his rucksack, tugged the straps open and groped inside for his mobile phone. He switched it on and pressed three nines and only then did he realise how much his body was trembling. His call was answered rapidly. He gave his name and address, as requested. Then he explained what he had found and did so in a voice he had to force to keep calm and clear. Directions proved impossible to give and so the man suggested that he return to the public highway, the B1252, between Garton-on-the-Wolds and Sledmere. 'A little nearer Sledmere,' he said, 'but really more or less halfway between. I'm wearing a baseball cap, white trousers, and I'll be standing at the roadside. There'll only be me, no one else about at all.'

The man walked back towards the road, back through the second wood, though no longer noticing the birdsong, back across the silent meadow of knee-high grass, back into the first wood and then followed the path which brought him to the rough track which ran from the road to Reed's Farm. He followed the side of the track where the going was easier, until after a walk of approximately two hundred yards, he reached the B1252; a narrow, pasty grey road in colour, driving a near straight path – though believed not to be of Roman origin – across the gentle undulation that was the Vale of York. He sat on the grass bank at the side of the road and waited. The marked police vehicle arrived within five minutes. Clearly, reasoned the man, it must have been on routine patrol in the vicinity. He raised his hand as it approached and, in response, the driver flashed the headlights once. The car halted beside the man and both officers, a male and a female, got out of the car.

'Mr Swannell?' the female officer asked. She was blonde

with blue eyes, high check bones, slender and long of leg; the type of girl, the man thought, that might have flirted with modelling before settling into a career.

'Yes.' Swannell stood as the officers approached him. 'Nigel Swannell. Nigel Swannell, at your service.'

Both officers made no attempt to conceal their amusement and approval of Swannell's archaism. They "read" him: late middle-aged, casually dressed, though appropriately so, solid shoes for country walking, lightweight and light coloured summer clothing, small red rucksack and, somewhat incongruously, they thought, a blue baseball cap with a logo of a modern drink currently being promoted within the young drinkers' market.

'You reported a body?' The male constable asked. He was dark haired, short for a constable.

'Indeed, indeed, I did.' Swannell glanced at the constables. A Norman and a Viking, clearly so, he thought, evidence that visitors to Britain's fair shores had brought with them more than their place naming and architecture; they had brought their genes as well. 'Not a sight I wish to see again. It's about a fifteen to twenty minute stroll from here.'

'Can we get the car nearer?' The male constable asked. He seemed to Swannell to be the senior of the two, certainly the leader, and had been behind the wheel of the police car.

'Only down this track.' Swannell indicated the track to Reed's Farm. 'As you see, it's only really suitable for Land Rovers and tractors.'

'Where does it go?'

'Go?' The man smiled. *It doesn't go anywhere*, he thought, *but it leads to a farm*, though he said, 'To Reed's Farm and it has steep banking all the way along, can't leave your car on the track without blocking it.'

The constables looked at each other and nodded. 'We'll walk from here,' the male constable said.

Swannell turned and walked down the track, retracing his route of earlier that afternoon: the path to the first wood; the meadow; the second wood and the stand of gorse surrounded by trees. Swannell stood at the edge of the gorse and said, 'There.'

'The flies?' the male constable asked.

'Yes…that's what attracted my attention. I do this walk every day, knew it had to be rotting flesh to attract flies like that, and living things do not venture willingly into gorse. I confess I pondered calling before I investigated but what would you have thought if I had phoned to report a swarm of flies? I might have made a case if I had emphasised it was a cloud of flies in the middle of a lot of gorse, but I didn't, and that's it.'

'I can understand that,' the male constable nodded, and thought Swannell reluctant to walk into the gorse.

'Well, I'll leave you.' Swannell switched his rucksack from one shoulder to the other. 'You have my name and address, but I doubt I can offer any information, the body wasn't there this time yesterday.' The constables looked at him as if to say, *how do you know?* and Swannell, anticipating the question said, 'No flies…there were no flies yesterday.'

'What do you do for a living, Mr Swannell?' The female constable asked.

Swannell swept the cap off his head, revealing a thin ring of silvery hair round an otherwise shiny, bald head and wiped sweat from his brow. 'I'm a composer.' He could not understand the relevance of the question, but answered it nonetheless. 'I was for many years, too many years, a banker…but the bank merged and downsized. I was given a generous redundancy package and a good pension and was thus able to devote my time to my first and only love – music. It can be tedious, scoring for many instruments: you can write all day and produce something which an orchestra would play in five minutes, but I love it...Working on my third symphony at the moment. I do this walk daily...seeking the muse.'

'Muse?'

'Inspiration, young sir, inspiration. In the summer it comes from birdsong, in the winter it comes from the wind and the rain. Well, today's walk has been delayed so I must press on.' Swannell turned and walked away and, as he did so, he heard the female constable say, 'Well, it only needs one of us.'

'I thought you'd say that,' Swannell heard the male reply, 'and I know which one of us it will be.'

In the end it was decided to hack the gorse away. Police Constable Nelson, whom Nigel Swannell had identified as being of Norman descent, had made slow and occasionally uncomfortable progress through the gorse towards the swarm of flies, had glanced once at the reason for the flies' interest and had returned to where Woman Police Constable Fletcher stood at the tree line making no attempt to conceal her mirth at Nelson's discomfort.

'Phone it in,' Nelson had said, 'it's as that guy says.' And WPC Fletcher had duly phoned "it" in, and while awaiting the Scene of Crime Officers, the CID officers and the police surgeon, the two police officers had set about ringing the entire stand of gorse with blue and white tape which they tied round the trees surrounding the gorse, so that the tape was strung from tree to tree to tree. Upon arrival, the turbaned Dr Mann had made the uncomfortable journey from the tree line to the swarm of flies and, like Constable Nelson an hour earlier, had glanced once at the corpse and had turned round. He told DCI Hennessey that his attendance had been a "formality" but he confirmed the person "life extinct" at 15.30 hours. Hennessey had duly noted the time in his notebook. He had then despatched the Scene of Crime Officers to the corpse to photograph the victim from all angles, using both colour and black and white film.

'How colourful,' had been Dr D'Acre's smiling observation when she arrived at the scene. 'I mean, the blue of the sky, the green of the leaf canopy of the wood, the yellow of the gorse and the police tape. What a pretty scene.'

Hennessey had returned the smile, but didn't reply. He had, by then, already viewed that which lay under the cloud of flies, albeit briefly, but sufficiently for him to see the crime scene as anything but "pretty". Dr D'Acre, showing more pluck and more spirit than Hennessey had been able to muster, or had observed in any other person that afternoon, then strode, black bag in hand, into the gorse. He watched as she knelt down, seemingly unconcerned by the flies, in order to collect data. She then stood and, carrying her bag, returned to where Hennessey stood.

'I would be inclined to agree with Dr Mann,' she said. 'Life is extinct.'

'Indeed.'

'Well, I have taken a rectal temperature and also the ground temperature. I've also collected these.' She held up a glass phial containing larvae. 'These will tell us when he died or at least when his body was left here. All we need now is the head and the hands.'

It was then that Hennessey realised he had no other option but to order the gorse be hacked away, down to its roots, and each bush probed for body parts, murder weapon, or anything else which may be relevant to the inquiry. He glanced up at the sky. 'Might just get this hacked away in the daylight we have left,' he spoke aloud.

'Well, I'll leave that to you.' Dr D'Acre placed the glass phial into her bag. 'If you could arrange for the body to be taken to York District Hospital, I'll start the PM immediately.'

'That's good of you, it's late in the day to be starting a

post-mortem.'

'It's a very fresh corpse, Detective Chief Inspector, probably still within twenty-four hours of death. There'll be an awful lot of blood somewhere...probably still tacky.'

'You don't think he was murdered here?'

'Hardly likely. I think...it's your department, of course, but it might be worth scouring the woodland that surrounds the gorse. You might find a pile of clothes and the rest of him, as well as some blood-soaked soil, but frankly, I don't think you will. It's a good place to hide a corpse. Even in winter when the gorse isn't in bloom, who would walk into it? Death by a thousand cuts if you did, though clearly somebody found it...the flies, I suspect?'

'Yes, fortunately for us the flies were spotted by a member of the public who realised the possible significance of flies in that quantity hovering over a small area of gorse. Many another person would not have given a second thought.'

'Good for that person, that corpse was hidden from view as determinedly as if it had been weighted down and left just below the dead low watermark in the Humber estuary. Some person – or persons – showed great determination in forcing their way so deep into the gorse. It would be like forcing your way into a stand of cactus or giant hogweed...well, perhaps not as bad as either of those two plants, but the point is made.'

'It is indeed, and had occurred to me, but said person, or persons, unknown, forgot or didn't know that the bluebottle can smell decaying flesh from two miles distant.'

'Yep...Christmas came early for them.'

'Pity to spoil it for them,' Hennessey grinned. 'They'll have to find something else to eat.'

'They're not eating it, they're laying eggs. The larvae I collected...the deterioration will be caused by primary invaders in the gut, eating from the inside out...small creatures like voles will help, as will birds of the ilk of crows and magpies, but principally, he will decay from the inside out.'

'Still, a pity to spoil their fun. Sergeant!'

'Sir!' The reply was crisp, sharp, attentive.

'Two constables and a stretcher please…better keep the body bag here, can't wrestle the corpse into a body bag in the gorse.'

'Very good, sir.' The sergeant turned away and beckoned to two white-faced constables to approach him.

'Well, I'll make my way back to the famous and fair. Who will observe for the police?'

'I'll ask Yellich.'

'Okay.' Dr D'Acre was a woman in her mid forties, short hair, dark but greying slightly, slender but strong with good muscle tone, evident to any observer in her walk and the ease with which she knelt and stood and carried a heavy bag…and with a trace of lipstick as her only makeup she was also clearly a woman who was surrendering to middle age with grace and dignity. 'I'll make my way back, commence the PM as soon as.'

Extra constables having been called in from other duties and equipped with tools and thick, heavy-duty gloves, Hennessey delegated the task of clearing the gorse to the sergeant and was not unimpressed by the way he did it. Two lines of white shirted constables were formed standing a line abreast and one line behind the other. The first line advance on the gorse with machete-like instruments drawn from Police stores, hacking at the base of each shrub, the severed shrub was then passed back to a constable in the second line who probed it for any item of relevance before placing it on a pile of similarly severed and examined bushes. It was clearly hot and back-breaking work, but the sergeant kept the constables working. The nearest thing to a break he allowed was once every 30 minutes when the leading line of constables handed the machetes to the following line. The two lines thus having exchanged roles, the work recommenced. It took fully three hours to clear the gorse.

Nothing was found.

Yet still the sergeant was not finished, for he ordered all the gorse that lay in isolated piles be gathered together in one central pile. 'Neater, you see, lads...leave it neat...make you feel better when you go off duty...better than leaving a mess behind.'

Hennessey added his voice of thanks, remarking that the job had had to be done and, even though nothing had been found, that was still a "result" in a sense. Tomorrow, he explained, tomorrow they will widen the search. 'Pleasant day in the woods for us tomorrow,' he added and raised a weary laugh from the exhausted officers.

There were four persons in the room: Dr Louise D'Acre, dressed in green disposable coveralls; the pathology laboratory assistant, the rotund and often jovial Eric Filey, also dressed in the same type of coveralls; Somerled Yellich, observing for the police, as Home Office procedures dictated, and similarly dressed. The fourth person lay on the right-hand most of the four stainless steel tables that stood in a row within the laboratory. Alone of the four persons, he was naked, save for a starched white towel which had been draped over his middle, and also alone of the four persons in the room, he was without head or hands. Dr D'Acre adjusted the anglepoise arm, which was attached to the ceiling above the dissecting table, so that the microphone on the end of the arm was about six inches above her head and in front of her. 'Do we have an identity?' She addressed Yellich.

'Not yet, ma'am.' Yellich raised his voice slightly so that it would carry clearly across the distance from where he stood against the wall.

'I see...so this is my reference then, sixteenth of this

month…"sixteenth inst.", please Valerie.' She looked at the corpse. 'Well, the body is that of a well nourished male, north-western European by racial category. He is middle-aged…probably. Say "probably middle-aged" please, Valerie.' She glanced at Yellich. 'No head means no teeth, no teeth means many things: it means no determining of ID by dental records and it also means no accurate ageing. With teeth we can determine a person's age at death to within twelve months.'

'I see,' Yellich responded. He thought his response weak but he knew he had to reply.

'We can determine an approximate age by other means, but we'll come to that.'

'Yes, ma'am.'

'Well, to continue, there are no marks of a distinguishing nature, no tattoos or birth marks on the anterior aspect. Mr Filey, if you'll get hold of the shoulders?'

Eric Filey stepped forward unhesitatingly and held the shoulders of the corpse as Dr D'Acre walked to the foot of the table and took hold of the ankles. 'Clockwise from your position, Mr Filey, on three…three…two…one…' And the corpse was turned over with a skill and apparent ease which impressed Yellich and which he knew had only been achieved through practice and by two people who understood each other perfectly. 'And no marks of a distinguishing nature on the posterior aspect.' Louise D'Acre spoke for the benefit of the microphone. 'While he's like this…' Dr D'Acre took a tape measure and placed it along the length of the spine and said, 'thirty-six inches.' She paused. 'Let's put him on his back again, please.' And the corpse was once again turned over in a smooth and efficient manner. Eric Filey draped the towel over the middle of the corpse and then retreated to the instrument trolley until his services were again required.

'So…age to be determined, and nothing as convenient as a

highly unusual tattoo or a distinctive birth mark...but we'll press on. He was a clean-living man, hygienically speaking. The soil that was attached to his body when he was brought in was superficial; the pores of his skin are clean. He wasn't a down-and-out and, like I said, he appears well nourished.' She tapped the table gently. 'Somebody somewhere will be missing this chap. Now...distinct discoloration is noted on the chest, stomach and the anterior aspect of the legs...that is hypostasis, it's caused by the blood settling due to gravity once the heart has stopped beating. That tells us a couple of things. It tells us that decapitation was not the cause of death. If he was alive when his head was cut off there would have been massive blood loss, so he died and his body lay, or was laid, face down for about twenty-four hours, possibly a little longer – it would take that amount of time for the blood to settle and solidify – and only then was he decapitated and we might presume that his hands were removed at the same time.'

'That's interesting, we can presume quite a lot from that,' Yellich mused.

'You think so?' Dr D'Acre smiled at him.

'Well, if the severing of his head was done after death...'

'Which it was.'

'Yes...then we can assume his death was not an accident and it was done to attempt to conceal his identity.'

'Well, I can think of no other reason to remove the head of a deceased person.'

'Nor can I...and if the head was removed to conceal the identity of the deceased, then so might the hands...'

'Ah,' Dr D'Acre raised an eyebrow, 'I see your thinking. The only way to identify someone by their hands is from their fingerprints.'

'Yes,' Yellich smiled. 'So he has a criminal record and the person or persons who did this knows that he has a criminal record. This smells of gangland...the effort that went into concealing his identity, the effort that went into concealing the corpse. This will make it a difficult case to crack...all clothing removed...all, if any, jewellery or wristwatch...'

'Well, any jewellery would have been attached to his hands or round his neck, but there is no impression of his having worn a wristwatch, no pale band of skin round his left wrist which we might expect at this time of the year, but I think you are correct. This death is very suspicious, though that is your area, mine is to tell you how he died.'

'And when...if you can, please, ma'am.'

'Mmm, I often have this conversation with Mr Hennessey. Strictly speaking, pathologists do not pronounce on the time of death, only the cause...though we may have allowed ourselves to be pushed into that role. Frankly, any simple or commonsense observation is as good an indication as anything I can tell you by means scientific. He, or she, died some time between the last confirmed sighting of them alive and the time their body was discovered, and that is about as accurate as you can safely get, but we'll see what we see, and we'll see if we can identify what he had for his last meal. I am making a standard, midline incision.' She turned to her left and reached for a scalpel and placed the scalpel at the base of the ribs of the corpse and drove a vertical line down towards the stomach. When over the stomach, Dr D'Acre drove one incision towards the left hip and another incision towards the right hip, thus creating a whole incision that looked like an inverted Y. She placed the scalpel in a tray of disinfectant liquid and, using only her hands, encased tightly in latex gloves, she peeled back the flesh from the incision in three distinct parts, thus exposing the stomach. 'Slightly bloated.' She pressed the stomach. 'This heat...the apparent age of the corpse...it's to be expected. You gentlemen may care to take a deep breath.' She plucked the scalpel from the tray of disinfectant and placed it on the wall of the stomach, turned her head to one side and punctured the stomach. The gas within escaped with a loud hiss. She stepped back, waving the air with her hand. 'I've smelled worse...much, much worse, but it's never pleasant, just varying degrees of unpleasant, from mildly unpleasant to unbearably unpleasant, and everything in between.'

Yellich exhaled and breathed in through his nose. He too had smelled worse. So had Eric Filey, thought Yellich, as he observed the man to scarcely flinch as the odour reached him.

Dr D'Acre forced a bold incision in the wall of the stomach and examined the contents. 'Well, he was a carnivore...had a substantial meal just before he died. Digestion will continue some time after death, and so, allowing for that, I would deduce that he was killed very shortly after eating what appears to be a main meal...an evening meal. He didn't masticate thoroughly, tended to swallow his meat in lumps rather than chewing them – never a good idea. Can't say from this when he died, and I shouldn't be doing this, but perhaps, thirty-six plus hours before he was found...or his body was found. "He" being in a better place by then. It's steak, beef anyway, the meal in his stomach, with vegetables, potatoes, peas, quite a heavy meal for this time of year...prawns too...a prawn cocktail to start...then the beef in whatever form, but it looks like a steak...but no dessert, no cheese, no fruit. He either didn't have a dessert by choice or he was chopped before he could properly finish his last meal. Very few victims of murder have notice of their death, and this gentleman was no exception. He was very relaxed up until the end...I would say, anyway. No scientific observation leads me to that conclusion, just logic. I cannot see this fellow eating a meal like this with a gun at his head, knowing that when he puts his knife and fork down, he'll be iced...just can't see it happening like that.'

'I can't either,' Yellich said, glancing at Eric Filey, who offered his tuppence worth by shaking his head as if saying, *I can't see it happening like that either.*

'A clean, self-respecting man who ate well.' Dr D'Acre didn't appear to Yellich to be addressing anyone in particular. 'He'll be missed alright, rapidly so, already so. Well...I will test for poison but I doubt I'll find a trace of any. He was eating vigorously up to the time of his death, that does not suggest poisoning. Let's have a look at his pump. Can I have the saw, please, Mr Filey?'

Eric Filey turned with near instantaneous obedience and opened a narrow drawer beneath the bench that ran the length of the wall of the laboratory, opposite the wall against which Yellich stood. He removed a small electrical saw with a circular blade, which he handed to Dr D'Acre. She mouthed "thank you" as she took the saw from him. She pressed the ON button and the blade spun round with a loud, whirring sound. 'Rather a good job they're dead,' Dr D'Acre smiled at Yellich. 'Wouldn't like to do this to living patients.'

'Indeed, ma'am.'

'And they're the only patients who don't complain either.' Still smiling at her joke, she placed the saw in the centre of the chest of the corpse and ran it down the chest from throat to abdomen, separating the ribs. She handed the saw back to Eric Filey, who began to clean the blade. Using brute force, Dr D'Acre then forced the ribs apart. 'Looks pretty healthy,' she observed. Taking a second scalpel, Dr D'Acre first made an incision across the right atrium, and then made a parallel incision on the wall of the right ventricle. With great and evident concentration, she made a third incision across the tricuspid valve. She took the heart, by then partially detached, and reversed it within the cavity and made a forth incision across the left atrium, a fifth incision was made on the anterior wall through the mitral valve and a final, sixth incision, was made through the aortic valve. The heart, thus freed of all attachments, was lifted carefully out of the chest cavity. She carried the heart to the working surface behind the dissecting table and, with a sharp knife, cut the heart into thin slices working from the aorta down. 'Well,' she said, turning to Yellich, 'a healthy heart, he didn't die of a heart attack. A little fatty…a little calcification in the pulmonary artery, but that isn't remarkable for a man of his apparent age…if I am right about him being in his middle years. So, let's look at his lungs.' Dr D'Acre took a long-bladed "brain knife" and passed it under the hilum with the blunt edge upwards. She then turned the knife, and so presenting the cutting edge to the hilum, severed it. She then lifted both lungs separately from the chest cavity and laid them on the dissecting board where she had moments earlier examined the heart. Dr D'Acre then, continuing to use the brain knife, cut the lungs from apex to base. The lungs fell away either side of the antero-posterior slice, enabling Dr D'Acre to consider the interior of the lungs. 'Fit man. Heavens, I've seen less healthy lungs in twenty-somethings.'

'Really?'

'Yes, really, Sergeant Yellich. I still think he's a middle-aged man…early middle years…late forties, but very healthy. Lived well and in comfort, showering or bathing each day. So let us turn to the determination of his age. No teeth…no skull to examine.' She glanced up at Yellich. 'I am so sorry, Sergeant, I don't seem to be of much help. I can't determine the cause of death, nor can I determine his age, save to say that he is adult and appears – I can only say appears – to be in his middle years. His height? Well, what did we say the length of the spine was?'

'About thirty-six inches, Dr D'Acre,' Eric Filey said from memory.

'Yes, that was it. That would make him about six feet tall in life.'

'It's still very useful, ma'am, healthy individual who lived well…six footer.'

'Approximately.'

'Yes…noted. Approximate height is…was, six feet. As you say, we can expect him to be reported missing, if he comes from this area. The police still don't have a national database of mis. pers., we rely on the good offices of the National Missing Persons Bureau for that.'

'I see…odd omission, but not for me to comment.'

Dr D'Acre scraped a sample of congealed blood into a small, clear plastic container and sealed the top. 'I'll send this to Wetherby, to the forensic laboratory there, ask them to test for poison and extract this gentleman's DNA profile. If he's on the DNA database, that will be of some considerable assistance to you.'

'It would indeed, thank you.'

'Well,' Dr D'Acre peeled off her latex gloves, 'that's all I can do here. The results will come back from Wetherby in a day or two. There won't be any poison in the sample, of that I am fairly certain; the meal he ate…he was too active before he died, and poisoning people's food went out with the Romans. My guess is that he suffered massive trauma to the head, that's what killed him…or similar…possible suffocation or strangulation, but there's no bruising about the body that would suggest that he put up a fight. He probably never knew what happened to him…a bullet or a blunt object impacting with his head while he was resting after his meal?'

'Or during it?' Yellich offered reverentially, diplomatically.

'Yes…no indication of a dessert, so possibly during it, as you say. I'll fax my report to you, for the attention of DCI Hennessey?'

'Please, ma'am, he's the senior officer in this inquiry.'

'Alright…it's as good as done.'

George Hennessey walked from the scene of the crime, the scene of the hacked gorse bushes that had been piled high by heavily perspiring constables, who had now left the area, and walked to the home of Nigel Swannell. Reporting the body and saying that he didn't see anything else that was suspicious was, he felt, not good enough, not good enough by half. Only a police officer can determine what was or was not suspicious. Hennessey enjoyed the stroll to Swannell's house. The intense heat of the afternoon had largely subsided although the sun was still fierce despite, by then, being low in the sky. A lovely, warm summer's evening was promised.

Nigel Swannell's residence revealed itself to be a red stone built house, squat in overall appearance with a roofline which was interrupted by a single chimney which seemed to Hennessey to be unusually, even unnecessarily, tall for the overall size of the building. It sat snugly a few feet back from the road, with trees at either side and a lawn to the front. The gate was painted a gloss black, which Hennessey felt was a warm colour, made warmer by the name of the house, Forester's Lodge, neatly painted in gold on the black background. A close inspection of the garden revealed no sign of children or animals. It was neat, well kept, perhaps even fastidious. It was a comparatively small garden but one which Hennessey saw as enjoying a great deal of hard manual attention. He leaned over the gate, searching for the latch, and finding it, released it and pushed the gate open. He walked up the narrow path to the heavy looking, metal studded front door of Forester's Lodge. He rapped the metal knocker that bolted to the door just beneath the letterbox. He turned as he waited for his knock to be answered and saw the view from the front of the house was that of pasture leading across to the road which ran between Sledmere and Garton-on-the-Wolds. The road, from Hennessey's vantage point, was hidden from view but its presence was betrayed by a red tractor that making sedate progress across the landscape from right to left and had accumulated a motor coach, a lorry and two cars in its wake. Beyond the road was more green pasture and occasional woodland which stretched to a low skyline in the distance, above which was a massive canopy of blue sky with just a wisp of cloud. The door was unlocked, Hennessey turned.

'Yes?' Nigel Swannell blinked at Hennessey.

'Police, Mr Swannell,' Hennessey smiled. He thought Swannell looked nervous. He was a slightly built man, his house was remote and he would be vulnerable to a team of youths or a single, well-built individual steaming over his threshold. Hennessey could understand his fear. He showed his ID.

'Ah…' Swannell smiled and visibly relaxed. 'Can't be too careful…the country can be a dangerous place, the picture postcard charm is very superficial. A crowd has a policing influence, it makes the city safer somehow…as we found today.'

'Yes…it's that which I came to see you about, sir.'

'Well, I don't know what else I can add but do come in. I don't get many callers, the company has been welcome.' Swannell stepped aside.

'Company?' Hennessey stepped into Forester's Lodge. It was, as he had expected of a stone building, cool inside and dark without being gloomy.

'Please…we'll go into the living room. Would you care for a cup of tea? I was about to make a pot. It really would be no bother, no bother at all.'

'Well, in that case, yes, thank you, that would be very welcome…it's been a hot day out there.'

'I can imagine. Please, take a seat.'

Hennessey sat in an upholstered chair with wooden armrests, not quite an armchair, but neither was it an upright. It accommodated the relaxed posture he assumed when sitting in a manner he found very comfortable. He read the room.

"Hard," in a word, he thought, *or "cold".* The room had a

low ceiling with protruding beams which seemed to glisten with the after effects of chemical treatment – presumably, Hennessey thought, for rot – but were otherwise naked, being neither painted nor varnished, and as such were not to his personal taste. The fireplace was elevated with an empty hearth. *Very neat*, he thought. In many houses in the Vale in this heat, the hearth would become a receptacle of anything inflammable to be burnt when the chill weather arrives, but not the hearth of Nigel Swannell's house. It was clear and clean, just a blackened iron grating inside a stone surround. The mantelpiece was similarly clean and unfettered, having just a small quartz clock placed upon it, centrally, almost as if the location of the clock had been measured to the millimetre. The clock, unsurprisingly, thought Hennessey, showed the correct time: 17.45 hours. Two prints of landscape paintings hung on the wall, both in heavy frames, one on either side of the fireplace, and both showing stormy scenes in winter. Not for Nigel Swannell was the cosy, 'chocolate box top' comfort of Constable's *Haywain* or *Boat Building on the Stour*. Clearly, Hennessey pondered, something in this man's psyche found an outlet in things cold, hard, precise…possibly even threatening…akin to the recently released, long serving convict who rapidly re-offends in order to be sent back "home". The floor was of polished floorboards with a rug of a busy red pattern covering the centre portion. The view through the window, set in a wall that Hennessey estimated to be equal in thickness to that of the distance between his wrist and elbow, was of the back garden. The back lawn was longer and wider than the lawn at the front, large enough, he thought, to accommodate a badminton court. It was bounded by flowerbeds and beyond the flowerbeds were shrubs which closed up to the wood beyond. A wooden fence, painted gloss black, like the front door, could be glimpsed between the shrubs and the trees. Like the front of the house, it was neat…very neat, and very tidy. It was the house of a single man, efficient, without the softness that would be breathed into it by a woman's touch, or the warmth that would be given into it by children or a pet dog or cat. Even a hamster in a cage, which might occasionally be allowed out to rummage round the floor, would, in Hennessey's view, be a welcome addition to this house.

Nigel Swannell returned with tea on a tray, a pot, milk, two cups and saucers, a spoon in each saucer and a small, matching pot containing sugar cubes. All very proper. He set the tray down on the coffee table which stood on the red rug, and then sat opposite Hennessey in the second, matching chair. 'Milk and sugar?'

'Just milk, please.'

Moments later, Hennessey was handed a cup of tea. It didn't contain sugar but for some reason he didn't understand, he picked up the spoon and stirred it anyway.

'So, how can I help you, Mr…?'

'Hennessey.'

'Like the brandy?' Swannell smiled.

'Different spelling, my name has an extra "e", but similar. Well, I understand you told my sergeant that you didn't see anything suspicious, other than the corpse? I have to say your deduction about the swarm of flies in a mass or gorse was…well, impressive.'

'It seemed obvious to me. I grew up near an area of gorse…it's impenetrable, nothing that would attract flies in that number would go into it, it was very suspicious.'

'It was also good of you to investigate, very determined.'

'Well, again, as I said to the other officer, I have a credibility to maintain. I didn't want to phone and report a cloud of flies.'

'We might…in fact, we would, have come out once you had explained your reasoning.' Hennessey sipped his tea. It tasted like hot water: it hadn't been allowed to infuse sufficiently in order to draw out the flavour. He sipped it anyway; it would not be appropriate to be churlish. 'I understand you walk on that path on a daily basis?'

'Yes...inspiration comes from walking...sights and sounds, but especially sounds.'

'Inspiration?'

'I am a composer, of classical music.'

Hennessey inclined his head in a gesture of respect and received an answering incline from Swannell which seemed to say, *acknowledgement gratefully received*, but in himself Hennessey found himself to be massively confused. This house, this room, the garden outside, the fastidious neatness, the everything-in-its-place "just so" efficiency was not, in his view, the home of an artist. He had been in the homes of artists both in a personal and professional capacity and all had been of the same ilk, clean, perhaps with attention given to basic hygiene, but tidy they were not – none of them. Nigel Swannell, he thought, was either an exception, and a rare exception at that, or a fantasist. An exception he could accept, a fantasist might be given to offering suspect information. So far though, Swannell's information had proved substantive, there could be no disputing that. Hennessey could only continue. 'So you saw nothing today that aroused your suspicion, other than the obvious as we have stated?'

'Nothing.'

'What about yesterday...or in any recent days?'

'Suspicious?'

'Out of the ordinary...a person never seen before, a motor vehicle never seen before...'

'Mmm...Mercedes-Benz parked on the track that leads to Reed's Farm. It was foreign in every sense, foreign make of car and foreign to the area. Never seen it before.'

'Interesting.' Hennessey reached for the notebook. 'A Mercedes-Benz, you say?'

'Yes, one of the more compact ones, not one of the great big sledges of cars that Mercedes manufacture.'

'I think I know the ones you mean. Colour?'

'Silver.'

Hennessey scribbled on his notepad.

'The owner didn't know the area.'

'No?'

'Wouldn't have parked on the track if he did. Reed is…curmudgeonly…the track is actually his property, any car parked there tends to get hooked up to his John Deere and dragged through a hedge and left in the wet field.'

'The wet field?'

'If you walk down the track towards the farm, the field to your left is a wet field, doesn't drain easily, though in this weather it's dry…the field to the right is a dry field.'

'I see.'

'Reed will allow folk to walk on the track and I can ride my bike.'

'A cycle?'

'A motorcycle with a sidecar. It's my lifeline to the outside world.' Then, as if reading Hennessey's mind, he said, 'It's parked behind the house. Can't see it from here.'

'Ah…'

'Anyway, it wasn't parked there long because Reed would have dragged it away.'

'When was that?'

'Two days ago. Yes, Monday…day before yesterday.'

'Time of day?'

'Oh, well, I take my walk in the early afternoon, so about that time.'

'Alright,' Hennessey scribbled in his notebook. 'Was there anything distinctive about the car?'

'Not that I noticed and no, I didn't get the registration number.'

'Too much to hope that you did,' Hennessey smiled. 'You had no reason to.'

'I didn't get close to the car…just noticed it and thought, *Jack Reed won't like that*, but the car clearly escaped the ignominy of being towed into the wet field. I am sure I would have heard about it if it had, or seen it. Cars that are towed into the wet stay there for days before the owner can sort a tow out. You see, if your car is stolen and left in a field, it's often the case that the farmer of that field will tow your car off and back to the road…'

'But in this case, it would be the farmer who towed it on to his land?'

'Exactly…so it takes time to organise a tow…think of days.'

'Alright, so not parked there long, and you didn't see the driver.'

'Not long…and no, I didn't.' Swannell similarly stirred his tea although Hennessey noticed that he too hadn't added sugar.

'What about previous days? Anything prior to Monday? Any strange vehicles or persons?'

'None that I saw, but I spend most of my day in my house…the walk in the afternoon…any provisions I need I buy in Sledmere. I don't drink, so I don't go out in the evening.'

'You must enjoy solitude?'

'I do actually…I find it well.'

Hennessey confessed that he, too, enjoyed a certain amount of solitude, but he thought Swannell's level of solitude would be too much for him to bear. He folded his notebook and slipped it into his pocket. 'Well, thank you, Mr Swannell.' He stood. 'If anything occurs to you that you think might be of interest to us...' He took a card from his wallet and handed it to Swannell, who by then was also standing. 'My name and workplace phone number.'

'I'll keep it safe.' Swannell accepted the card and leaned down to place it on the coffee table next to the tray. 'And yes, of course I'll phone if anything occurs to me.'

Hennessey walked out of Swannell's house, noting how diplomatically and sensitively and politely did Swannell wait until he had reached the gate before closing the door with a gentle click. As a police officer, he was rarely a welcome visitor to people's houses and, as such, it was his experience that doors were slammed behind him the instant he stepped back across the threshold. Consequently, he appreciated Swannell's gesture. He walked further on, back to where he had parked his car, fortunately not on the track to Reed's farm. So, he pondered, a male corpse...without head and hands...would probably never have been found save for Swannell's clever deduction. The result of the post-mortem he would doubtless learn tomorrow. A strange car, a distinctive Mercedes seen in the area a few days – probably the day before – the body was dumped; somebody doing a recce? After all, he further pondered, it would be highly unlikely for someone to drive around with a headless and handless corpse in the boot of a car, looking for somewhere to dump it. It was a possible lead. He reached the track which allegedly led to the allegedly ill-tempered Mr Reed and wondered whether to call on him. He decided to postpone visiting the farmer with the penchant for towing cars into the wet field. The man would have to be visited, but that visit could wait until the morrow. He walked back to where he had parked his car and drove back to York.

Unusually for him, very unusually, he found he enjoyed the drive.

Chapter Two

Thursday, 9th of July, 09.10 – 12.20 hours
*in which Hennessey meets aggression and usefulness in equal
quantities and Yellich visits another time and another place.*

Hennessey relaxed in his chair, leaning back, as he listened to
Yellich's delivery. He cradled a mug of tea in his hands, occasionally looking out of his office window at the walls at
Micklegate Bar. It was early still, but the walls were already
thronged with tourists. Despite the occasional glance to his
left, his mind was focused on Yellich, his attention never wan-
dered.

'So…' he said, when Yellich had finished and he too sat
back in his chair, 'so a clean and good living man, topped when
he was halfway through dinner. No evidence of cause of death
with what Dr D'Acre had to work with. Astounding, isn't it?'

'Sir?'

'The head…such a small part of the human body, yet it
contains so much information for the pathologist and hence
ourselves. It's surprisingly disabling when we don't have a
head.'

'My dentist said pretty much the same thing once, when I
was getting an ear-bashing for going too long without a
check-up. "The mouth is such a small part of the human body,
just two rows of teeth and the gums that hold them. You can
get that in an ordinary envelope, yet there is an entire branch
of medical science devoted to it…ought to show you the
importance of dentistry," sayeth he. "You don't have entire
branches of medical science devoted to the hand or the foot,
yet both are larger than the mouth." He really rammed the
point home. He's a good chap, we are lucky to have him.'

Hennessey smiled. 'Yes, it's been a while since I've reclined
in a dentist's chair, must rectify that. But the mouth is such a

goldmine of information for us…we haven't got that in this case. No skull to reconstruct or impose photographic images on, no indication of his facial appearance…bearded or clean-shaven. It just shows how much we depend on the head for.'

'Indeed, boss.'

'Well, I visited the member of the public who phoned us, Mr Swannell.' Hennessey then related his impression of Swannell, claiming to be an artist yet living in such a neatly kept house. 'More like the home of a so called "control freak" than an artist,' he said. 'The sort of house where the occupant would run his fingers along the tops of doors to check for dust, but he seemed genuine.' He then told Yellich about the Mercedes-Benz seen in the lane.

'Could very well be relevant, skipper,' Yellich mused. 'A Merc…ties in with the good living that Dr D'Acre drew attention to. The corpse was very clean…no dirt ingrained in the pores of the skin…the meal…'

'Prawn cocktail, followed by steak.'

'Yes, boss, no down-and-out with junk food, if anything at all, in his stomach. He…this man, was clean and ate well. The Mercedes ties in very well with that.'

'So, what's for action?'

'Sweep the woodland around the crime scene…the constables will enjoy that…take the job seriously, but it's better than some such areas I can think of.'

'Yes, I know what you mean. Have to spare a lucky few from pounding the streets of the famous and faire for a morning out in the country. I am sure they won't object.' Hennessey grinned.

'Sure they won't either, sir.' Yellich returned the grin. 'A policeman's lot is not such an unhappy one at times.'

'Anything else, you think?'

'Can't think of anything, boss.'

'Can't you?' Hennessey raised an eyebrow.

'I think you can, sir.'

'Well, I want to go and talk to the farmer, Mr Reed, he lives locally, he may have seen something. Doubt he'll be able to confirm the silver Mercedes because by all accounts, it would have wound up axle deep in mud…well, perhaps not at this time of the year, but well off the track anyway, if he had seen it. But the woodland and the gorse is on his land, he'll have noticed stranger activity if anyone will.'

'Good point, boss.'

'And anything else?'

'Mis. pers., sir?'

'Yes. Exactly. Let's do that now.' Hennessey reached forward and picked up the phone on his desk and jabbed a four figure internal number. Yellich listened to one side of the conversation. 'DCI Hennessey. Any missing person reported within the last forty…no, seventy-two hours? Male, six feet in height approx, possibly moneyed…no down-and-out here.' Hennessey cupped the phone and said, 'Checking.'

Yellich nodded. Then he saw Hennessey smile and give the "thumbs up" sign. He watched as Hennessey scribbled on his notepad and listened as he said, 'Thank you, indeed. Well, well,' he said to Yellich as he replaced the phone with a gentleness which Yellich had observed before. 'We might have a result.'

'Really? I had feared it might have been an out of town number.'

'So had I, but one Benjamin Tansey, aged 42, was reported missing yesterday. He was reported by his mother…height given as approximately six feet.'

'His mother? At the age of 42?'

'Yes…at the age of 42…don't read anything into that, Yellich, not at this stage. Address out on the Shipton Road, beyond Skelton.'

'Moneyed…it's tying in…beyond Skelton is big money.'

Hennessey tore the page of his notepad. 'Go and visit, find out what you can.'

'Yes, boss.' Yellich stood.

'I'll organise the search of the woodland and call on the ill-tempered Mr Reed. Rendezvous here…say, 14.00 hours.'

'Very good, boss. 14.00 hours.'

Leaving the search of the woodland surrounding the gorse, in which the body was found, in the capable hands of twenty constables and a sergeant, George Hennessey enjoyed the pleasant stroll to Reed's Farm.

The farm itself revealed itself to be a clearly successful venture. The house was neat looking, evidently freshly painted with a small, well-kept rose garden to the front. The outbuildings by the side of the house seemed, to Hennessey's eye, to be solid and well maintained. The cars beside the house, a large Volvo and a small VW, said "his" and "hers", and both were less than two years old. The equally recently built Land Rover and the two similarly equally recently built John Deeres that stood in front of the outbuildings contributed further to the overall impression that Hennessey was calling on serious money. No struggling hill farmer here. This was farming on a well-organised and fully mechanised scale. It is the sort of farm, Hennessey thought as he opened the front gate of the path which led to the door of the farmhouse, that makes farming an industry. He pressed the doorbell. It rang a harsh, jarring sound, more akin, he thought, to an alarm bell than a doorbell. There was no immediate response to his pressing of the bell and he was about to press it again when he heard a sound from within the house…a door being opened and shut again, slammed almost, and a heavy footfall approaching. The front door was flung open by a burly man dressed in a vest and shorts, grey hairs protruding in a mass from behind the vest. A pair of piercing eyes burned angrily into Hennessey's from beneath a perspiring, domed forehead.

'What!' The man demanded. It seemed to Hennessey that he was used to intimidating people.

Hennessey held the pause. He put his hand slowly inside his jacket pocked and produced his ID. 'Police,' he said, calmly.

'Well…what?' The man's tone seemed to Hennessey to be softened by curiosity.

'Are you the owner of this farm, a Mr Reed?'

'Yes.' Again, the tone was aggressive. 'About the body?'

'Which body?'

'The body that was found yesterday.'

'What do you know about it?'

'That the body was found in the gorse between the first and second wood.'

'How do you know that?'

'This is the country. Are you from the city? Ha!' Reed sneered with obvious derision at a "townie".

Hennessey had met such an attitude before in country folk who think that they are better in some way than city dwellers.

'Well, this is the country, in the country your business is everybody else's business and everybody else's business is your business. Not much that goes on is missed in the country. You might not see eyes looking at you but you're being watched…believe me…you're being watched.'

'So I have heard.'

'Well, all that police activity yesterday. You had quite an audience, believe me. So, of course, I heard about it.'

'I see. So who owns the land on which the body was found?'

'It's common land, so…North Yorkshire County Council. It's kept as a hide for game. The wood is where the foxes and badgers live. I run a highly mechanised farm but I know the value of not destroying nature with intensive, heavily chemically-dependent farming. I own, and I mean own, the 800 acres which surround the wood. Really it's just one wood despite being called first and second wood...and I benefit from it and I protect the game there. Had some trouble with badger baiting some years back...very heavy boys...they got away with it because they can intimidate people, but I can be heavy too. We knew who they were, we visited one night and put them all in hospital and shot their dogs.'

'Not a very animal loving act, for an animal lover.'

'Believe me, once a dog has been set to fighting badgers as part of a pack, it's no good. It's likely to turn on anything, especially if it's with other dogs. My workers live in tied cottages and one or two have children. Believe me, no owners to control them, those dogs were dangerous. We did the sensible thing there.'

'Don't remember that being reported.'

'It wasn't. The hospital reported the assaults to the police but those baiters were wise enough not to want to make a complaint...so when they left the hospital after a few weeks...'

'Weeks!'

'Weeks. When they left hospital, they picked up their jobs and carried on. If they had made a complaint, I would have made sure they never worked again, not in the Vale anyway. After that, the badgers became known as Reed's badgers and they got left alone.'

'Lucky them.'

'Aye...so that's what it's like here, so that's how I know about the body in the gorse.'

'I see.' Hennessey paused. 'I understand the track which leads to your farm is your property?'

'As opposed to being public highway? Yes, it is. Let people use it like that fella in the lodge house...and dog walkers and the like, but yes, it's mine.'

'It's quite narrow. You won't be happy with people parking

their cars on it?'

'Well, like the badger baiters, folk who park their cars on the lane do so only once...I need that track kept open at all times. This is a working farm and I don't take prisoners.'

'Yes,' Hennessey growled, 'that's the impression I have.' Hennessey thought Reed to be a man of his own vintage, mid-fifties. He was about Hennessey's size too, certainly Hennessey's height, probably heavier in terms of weight. 'So I take it you didn't notice a silver Mercedes-Benz parked on the track at any time in the last few days?'

'No...I didn't notice any such, nor was any such reported to me by my workers or my wife. If it had been, I would have got into one of the John Deeres and towed it off the track...so if it was there, it was only for a matter of minutes, not long enough to be noticed.'

'So things are missed in the country?'

'Never said they weren't. I said, not much is missed in the country. So, of course, some things happen that are not seen. I mean, somebody dumped a body in the gorse and did that without being seen. Mind you, I can tell you that that would have been done at night. Couldn't have done that during the day without being seen...not a chance.'

'That's of some help.'

'And it was dumped the night before it was found.'

'Yes...we have that information already, thanks.'

'The flies?' Reed again smirked. 'You might think that that was a clever observation of that guy, Swannell, but that's a townie for you. Any countryman would have realised the significance of it and that tells you something else as well...'

'Oh?'

'Yes...tells you that the people who did that, who dumped the body in the gorse, are townies. Only a townie would try to hide a body in the gorse this far out in the country and think it a perfect place to hide a body. A countryman would have realised that a decaying body would attract flies. Might as well put up a sign saying "Here be murder victim". Might have got away with it if they had dumped the body in one of those areas of waste land in the city…with housing estates around it…possibly then nobody would have given the swarm of flies a second glance, but out here, the significance of that would not be missed. No, no question…you're looking for townies.'

'Thank you,' Hennessey smiled. 'That has helped us.'

'Well, if that's all, I've got to get back to my accounts.' Reed slammed the door in Hennessey's face.

'And a good day to you, too, sir,' said Hennessey to the front door of Reed's farmhouse.

The man stood on the wall, sun hat, brightly coloured clothing, camera, drawing no attention to himself. Just another tourist. He turned from looking at Nunnery Lane, to the grassed area on the other side of the wall, just beneath him, to children playing, to one child whom he had been slowly getting to know over the years. His eyes and the boy's eyes met and they each raised a hand in greeting, just a second or two, then the boy's attention returned to the game, and the man turned his own attention back to Nunnery Lane. *Looks like his father. Taking after him already*, he thought, *but it's that stance, that bearing…that comes from his grandmother*.

Yellich, similarly, felt he was calling on money and he, too, realised that he wasn't just calling on money, he was calling on big money, serious shekels, big bucks, a pile of folding green high enough to jump off. The house was called Sheringham, which Yellich knew to be a small town on the north Norfolk coast, but felt that the name worked quite well as a name for a house, it having a solid, yet homely and comforting ring to it. The house itself stood in grounds that Yellich thought to be about the size of a football pitch and which were landscaped and clearly closely tended; a lawn with a small fountain in the middle stretched in front of the house. Yellich was instantly in two minds about the fountain, modest as it may be. On the one hand he appreciated the calming and soothing affect of the clean, running water, yet was equally annoyed by the selfish squandering of it. Britain has no shortage of water in the winter months when excess water is allowed to drain from reservoirs and into the river system and thence out to sea, but it is also an island that can slide rapidly into drought conditions during the summer. Britain, and particularly the Vale of York, were, at that particular time, not near drought conditions, but were in a situation where every drop helps. As he drove up the drive towards the house, the balance of Yellich's mind in respect of the fountain tipped towards condemnation of it.

He absorbed the image of the house as he approached it. The drive ran up the side of the grounds and curved in front of the house where it widened into a turning circle so that, as Yellich approached Sheringham, he viewed it not through his windscreen, but was obliged to turn his head at forty-five degrees to view it through the passenger door window. It was, he saw, a low, almost squat, rambling building of late nineteenth century vintage. It had a busy roof line, beloved of Victorians, with the frontage of the house complicated by turret rooms and dormer windows and a vast porch which protruded, rudely, in Yellich's view, a needlessly long way out, to the point that might be said to "invade" the turning circle in front. That the building was well kept was plain to Yellich. Like the garden, the house enjoyed close attention, not a tile out of place and the brown paint which covered the entire building would not need replacing for another five years, and the varnish upon the door and window frame seemed to Yellich to be equally freshly applied. The double garages set back, separate from the side of the building would doubtless contain a Rolls Royce, if not a brace of them. It seemed to Yellich to be that sort of property.

Yellich halted his car in front of the main door of the house and got out, his shoes crunching loudly on the gravel as he did so. Other than the sound of his shoes upon the gravel, all about him was silence. It was also entirely still. No sound, no movement, a vast garden, a vast house, a vast blue sky above, a relentless sun beating down causing a heat haze to rise from the stones around the fountain which, in turn, caused the cascading water to shimmer, curiously, hypnotically. Yellich walked to the front door and pulled the bell pull. He heard the jangle of bells echoing in the interior of the building.

The door was opened by a maid. She was middle-aged, slender, black. She looked at Yellich but gave nothing away, nothing by speech, nothing by body language. Her eyes were impenetrable, glassy. Yellich felt the urge to say something: he was clearly expected to state his business, but then he thought, *no...no...I'm the cop here...I am the authority. The only no-go areas for the police in Britain is Ministry of Defence land, and that's only because they have their own police force.* So he waited.

And waited.

And waited.

The maid didn't even blink. She stood there, in the threshold, impassive.

Waiting.

Eventually Yellich gave up and said, 'Police.'

'Yes, sir?' The maid's answer was prompt, efficient and Yellich saw her smile, slightly so, in the knowledge that she had won the game.

'Mrs Tansey...she reported her son as missing.'

'Yes, sir.'

'Is she at home?'

'Yes, sir.'

Another pause.

Again Yellich relented. 'May I see her?'

'If you'd like to step this way, sir.' Yellich detected a slight West Indian accent. She had, he reasoned, lived in the UK for some considerable length of time or had been born in the UK of West Indian parents who had emigrated to Britain but had retained their native accent. She led Yellich into a wide entrance hall that Yellich found pleasantly cool, yet oppressive, largely caused, he thought, by the ceiling, which he felt to be too low for his taste. He estimated the ceiling to be slightly out of reach, but only slightly, so slightly that he fancied that if he jumped up he could touch it with ease. The walls, too, had an oppressive quality about them, being panelled. The panelling was not only heavy but was stained with a particularly dark shade of varnish. Doors led off to the right and left and directly opposite the front door via which Yellich had entered the house. The light source came from two small windows either side of the front door. It was very cell-like.

'Please wait here, sir.' The maid spoke without glancing at Yellich, walked to a door to the right of the entrance to the house, opened it, allowing Yellich a brief glance of a dark and oppressive seeming hallway beyond, before shutting the door behind her slowly, but yet with a loud click. Very cell-like, indeed. The hallway had no decoration, no paintings or prints to ponder and so, for the sake of looking at something in order to pass the time, because he knew, intuitively, that the maid would be some minutes returning, he turned and looked out of one of the small windows at the grounds in front of the house. There, at least, was a sense of life, a sense of space. As he looked out across the lawn, he saw a man, clearly a gardener, emerge from a gap between two rhododendron bushes to the left of the garden, pushing a wheelbarrow in front of him. He pushed the barrow away from the house, over the lawn, and then turned into a similar gap and thus disappeared from

Yellich's view. But he had seen enough; middle-aged, like the maid, slender, like the maid though a little taller, and also, like the maid, he was black Afro Caribbean. Yellich thought, *man and wife*.

The maid returned, by which time Yellich guessed he had been kept waiting for ten minutes, possibly even longer. It was, he thought, a long time in such circumstances, during which Yellich's anger rose in direct correspondence to his patience receding.

'Mrs Tansey will see you now.'

'She will, will she?' Yellich snarled through gritted teeth. 'I am not here to ask her favour or permission.'

'No, sir.' The maid spoke calmly; she was clearly not at all intimidated by Yellich. She had, he thought, a rather detached air about her that was not wholly healthy. 'This way, please.'

The maid led Yellich down the hallway he had previously glimpsed. It was lighter than the entrance hall, having large windows to the right and doors to the left. He thought it a curious design for a house, which a family might wish to use to create a home. It was, he thought, a corridor more than it was a hall, windows to one side, heavy-looking wooden doors to the left. It was cave-like too, he thought. It did, indeed, feel like he was walking in a cave, despite the presence of the windows and the generous view they afforded of the front garden, in which, at that moment, lurked a middle-aged gardener. The maid stopped at the door at the end of the corridor, opened it and led Yellich into a square area, similar to the entrance hall in which his patience had ebbed. Stairs, wide and angular, led up from this second space to the first floor. Again, there was the same heavy panelling, the same dark shade of varnish, in addition there was also a pleasant, homely smell of wood polish, as if the maid, in her duties had not yet reached the entrance hall, but would doubtlessly get there before the day was out.

The maid took the stairs in a sprightly step, which impressed Yellich. She was clearly lithe for her years, housework had kept her very fit, very healthy. He was reminded of an article he had read in a magazine which told of the extraordinary amount of physical exercise done in a single day by the average housewife with a family, kneeling, bending, lifting, scrubbing, polishing, shopping...it was something phenomenal...something in the order of a five mile hike with a rucksack each day. Watching the maid sprint up the stairs, he could well accept the veracity of the article. The maid walked along a corridor on the first floor and stopped at a door. She paused and knocked twice.

Silence.

The maid stood still and waited. Yellich, keenly observing, did likewise.

'Come.' The tone was haughty, so Yellich thought, as was the pause between the knock and response. Black servants and an imperious attitude that belonged to an earlier era. Yellich was prepared to dislike Mrs Tansey before even meeting her.

The maid opened the door and pushed it open. 'Police officer to see you, ma'am.' The maid's knees buckled in a slight curtsey.

'Thank you, Sally.' The voice was of the manner that Yellich understood to be called "received pronunciation", like a BBC newscaster, the sort of voice that the blokes in the taproom of the Gun Inn would describe as "posh". 'Show the gentleman in.'

Sally stepped aside and Yellich entered the room.

It was an upstairs drawing room. Yellich scanned it quickly; dark brown carpet, burgundy red leather Chesterfield-style settee and two matching chairs, heavily stained panelling on the walls, leaded windows which looked out onto the evidently park-like expanse of the rear garden, beamed ceiling, a light in the centre of the ceiling was supplemented by tall lamps with generous shades in each corner of the room. Mrs Tansey,

Yellich presumed it was she, was sitting in the armchair which faced the door of the room and was thus able to glance at Yellich without turning her head. For glance was all she did, a glance was all her visitor was worth before her attention at once returned to the newspaper which lay open across her lap. She was, Yellich noted, a slender woman, grey hair, cut short, spectacles, a white blouse, red skirt, dark nylons, red shoes. He thought her perhaps mid to late sixties and was neither elegant nor slatternly in her dress, though he sensed that she could, with little effort, be very much of either, should she wish to put her mind to it. Sally, the maid, withdrew and closed the door behind her with a loud click.

Silence descended. Again. Yellich found himself waiting…again. It was clearly a house which expected any visitor to speak first. On this occasion, Yellich felt disinclined to play games. He had lost to Sally the maid; he had no chance against "m'lady", engrossed as she clearly was in that morning's edition of the *Daily Telegraph*.

'DS Yellich, ma'am,' he said. 'Micklegate Bar Police Station, York.'

Upon hearing him, the woman looked up and smiled and politely folded her newspaper and laid it on the small wooden table that stood beside her chair, as if rewarding him for introducing himself. 'How can I help you, Mr Yellich?'

'I understand you have reported your son as being a missing person? You are Mrs Tansey?'

'I am…Mrs Annabella Tansey. Please, do take a seat.' She opened her hand in an invitation to sit on the settee, adjacent to her, and separated from her by a heavy looking coffee table which stood between the settee and the chair. He was clearly not invited to sit in the armchair opposite her; he was not being invited to assume a seat which implied equality of rank.

'Thank you.' He walked across the deep pile of the carpet and sat on the Chesterfield settee causing the leather to

squeak as he did so. The noise caused him to keep his movement to a minimum thereafter. He sensed that Mrs Tansey
was amused by his insecurity. 'You reported your son as a
missing person?'

'I did...just to be cautious...I am sure he's safe and sound
somewhere, tucked up with a floozy, no doubt. He is a grown
man. I'll let you know when he returns. I am just being
safe...erring on the side of caution, as my late husband would
have wanted me to do. I presume you are just visiting me as a
matter of routine?'

'Not quite, I am afraid, Mrs Tansey.'

The woman gasped, 'Benjamin!'

'It's too early to be alarmed, Mrs Tansey...but I have to
inform you that a body has been found.'

'A body?'

'Yes...the identification is...well, it hasn't been made yet,
which is one of the reasons I ask you not to be alarmed; but it
is a male body of adult but indeterminate age...the height
appears to be about six feet or about one hundred and eighty
centimetres.'

'Ugh!' She held out her hand palms outwards, or vertical,
in the universal gesture of refusal. 'I do so hate metric...I do
so hate anything to do with Europe. So please, let's keep it to
the lovely old Imperial measurements. Six feet.'

'Very well. The body is that of a six foot tall male...very
recently deceased and found locally...which means nothing.'

'Nothing?' She looked at Yellich in a manner which was
penetrating, quizzical, "headmistressy". 'What do you mean,
nothing?'

'It means it implies nothing...no significance can be drawn
from where a body is found in itself, any significance will be
revealed when the body is identified.'

'Ah...' Mrs Tansey looked relieved. 'So what you are saying
is that the body could have come from anywhere?'

'Yes, exactly. Being found in our patch doesn't mean to say he lived in this locality. I mean, for example, how often have you read about someone driving from the south or west of England with a body in the boot of their car heading to Cumbria in the Lake District? Believe me, those beautiful lakes contain a lot of dark secrets.'

'I can imagine. So the body may not be that of my son?'

'No.' Yellich remained stone-faced. He wanted to reassure Mrs Tansey and yet, at the same time, he also felt he ought to prepare her for the worst. 'But the corpse is recent...death occurred a matter of hours ago.'

'Hours! You have been quick.'

'By hours I mean anything up to 72 hours. After 96 hours we start talking in terms of days. But you reported your son missing yesterday, he seems to fit what description we have and the timescale is also right. I mean, if the corpse was badly decomposed...'

'Please, this is my son we are talking about.'

'I'm sorry...but we may not be talking about him. What I mean is that if your son was known to be alive two days ago...'

'Which he was.'

'Then if the corpse was decomposed, we would know it couldn't be him. So, we would like to eliminate the possibility that the body is that of your son.'

'So would I!' She sat back in her chair. 'So would I. So would I. So would I.'

'So...' Yellich reached for his notepad and pen, causing the shiny leather of the Chesterfield to squeak as he did so, 'the thing we need is something of him...'

'Him!'

'Sorry, I didn't put that very well.'

'That's an understatement, young man. Would you like to try again?'

'Yes...thank you. What will confirm that the corpse is that

of your son is a DNA match.'

'Yes...I have heard of such.'

'If he has a comb, with his scalp hair...unwashed clothing.'

'I am sure I can let you see his room...you may remove anything you care to remove, within reason, of course, with the purpose of obtaining his DNA and with only that purpose.'

'Of course.'

Annabella Tansey reached a slender hand and a slender finger towards a brass button set in the wall and pressed the button. 'It doesn't sound in here,' she said, 'but Sally will hear it. Sally and Henry came from the West Indies with us...we brought them back...they're such darlings, utterly invaluable.'

Yellich thought, *you make them sound like possessions*, but said, 'So you lived in the West Indies?'

'Yes. We owned a sugar cane plantation...more fun than a sugar beet plantation in windswept East Anglia although the product is identical.'

'Really? Never knew that.'

'Most people don't. Most people assume that there is a difference between sugar beet and sugar cane. In fact, after processing, the product is identical.'

'Well, well. I had always assumed there was a difference.'

'Only in the source, not the final product. But yes...we had over seven hundred acres of sugar cane. We sold each crop in a semi-processed state. We crushed the cane on site to extract the molasses and sold the molasses to a brokerage and they sold it on to the sugar manufacturers who refined it in the west, close to the market. We didn't make a dreadfully good living, not really. We had the house, of course, dating from the eighteenth century when the plantation was worked by slave labour, we had cars...servants...we joined the golf club with other English ex-pats...but we also had high overheads. The hands had to be paid; the machinery needed servicing. You have to put in to get out like any form of farming, like any form of business really, but we were putting in as much as we were getting out in order to keep up the lifestyle. We really made our money by selling up. We bought it during a slump in the sugar industry and sold it in a boom. Bought it, worked it for ten years, then sold it for five times the amount we paid for it.'

'Five times?' Yellich gasped. 'In a ten year period?'

'Yes,' Mrs Tansey smiled. 'Not bad, you'll agree?'

'Well, yes. My own house has doubled in value in about six years, and I thought that was good, but a five-fold increase in just ten years...'

'Yes, we were not displeased either. We bought this property with the proceeds and I still have much in investment accounts. But Sally and Henry were our principal servants on Sheringham.'

'Sheringham?'

'It was...still is the name of the plantation, named by the man who carved it out of virgin jungle in the seventeen hundreds...he was a Norfolk man.'

'I noted the name of this house.'

'Yes...the house is not named after the town on the Norfolk coast, but after the plantation in the West Indies which was named after the town, so the name has come back to Britain.'

'I see...that makes sense. I did wonder at the name on a house in Yorkshire.'

'And Sally and Henry came too.'

'They were able to emigrate?'

'Oh, heavens, no,' Mrs Tansey looked shocked, 'they came as our guests...technically speaking...probably shouldn't have told you that.'

'Probably you shouldn't.'

'Well, if the immigration people come to call, I will insist they are my guests. They don't claim state benefit and they don't want to be housed. They're paid in cash each week…minimal wage of course…but then free accommodation is theirs plus all the food they can eat. That's not exploitation.'

'But they have no rights.'

'None,' again she smiled, 'as it should be. The relationship between employer and employee should be one of mutual respect with each knowing their place. I appreciate the concept of *noblesse oblige*, Mr…'

'Yellich.'

'Ah, yes. And while it pleases me to employ Sally and Henry, it is incumbent upon me to ensure their continued well-being. We don't need silly government rules.'

'And if it comes to pass that it no longer pleases you to employ Sally and Henry?'

'Then they become…what's the term we hear so much of these days? Those people that sneak through the tunnel and cling to the sides of ferry boats?'

'Illegal aliens?'

'Yes, illegal aliens and I dare say they'll be put on the first plane to Jamaica. They know that of course and so ensure I find little fault about their work. They have each Sunday off and a two week holiday in June. Unpaid, of course.'

'Of course.'

There was a polite, reverential knock on the door. Just two taps. Then silence.

'It's one of the reasons I choose to spend my time in the upstairs drawing room, Mr Yellich. It is the rule of this house, as in many other houses in England, that servants may enter downstairs rooms without knocking but must knock on the doors of upstairs rooms and wait to be called to enter. I believe it was established in the eighteenth century.' She paused, raised her head slightly and with a slightly raised voice called, 'Come.'

The door opened. Sally entered, curtseyed and said, 'You rang, ma'am?'

'Yes, thank you, Sally. A strange request...'

'Yes, ma'am?'

'Can you go to Mr Benjamin's room and obtain a strand of his hair from his comb or hairbrush or similar.'

'His hair, ma'am?'

'Yes, for the police officer.'

'If you don't mind, Mrs Tansey, I would like to obtain it myself. I know what I am looking for.'

'I do mind. I dislike the idea of you wandering about the rooms and corridors of Sheringham but I will relent...I dare say it is in my interest.'

'It is...really. It's in both our interests.'

'But you may not search the room as such, and I want Sally to accompany you and remain with you at all times.'

'Very well.' Yellich stood, not displeased to be leaving Mrs Tansey's presence.

Yellich followed Sally along the upstairs corridor. Again he felt something oppressive about the house, again he felt as though he was walking in a cave. Sally stopped at a door and knocked on it. She turned and smiled at Yellich and said, 'Habit, sir.'

'Ah...' Yellich returned the smile.

'Even though Mr Benjamin, he's not here, I still knock.' She opened the door and walked into the room. It was a bedroom. A double bed stood against the right-hand wall, a chest of drawers and a wardrobe stood beside it. A settee sat under the window which, like the room in which Yellich had met the lady of the house, also looked out onto the rear garden. Encouragingly, Yellich thought, encouragingly in the extreme, the bedroom had a bathroom en suite.

'Does anybody else use the bathroom?' Yellich turned to

Sally.

'No, sir.'

'When did Mr Benjamin use it last?'

'Well, he last slept in the bed on Sunday night, sir.'

'I see.' Yellich strode towards the bathroom. 'When was it cleaned last?'

'It hasn't been properly cleaned since he left, sir.' Sally stood in the centre of the bedroom, hands clasped in front of her.

'Excellent.' Yellich strode to the bathroom and looked first in the plughole of the bath and found, to his delight, a mass of hair. He took a self-sealing cellophane sachet from his pocket and picked up the hair from the plughole and placed it in the sachet. He turned to the washbasin, to the shelf beside the washbasin and found thereon a gentleman's hairbrush. He picked it up and walked to the door and held up the brush. 'Is this Mr Benjamin's hairbrush?'

'Yes, sir.' Sally annoyingly curtseyed as she answered. Yellich thought Sally was probably just old enough to be his mother and yet she stood there curtseying. Sheringham, he felt, was clearly a house from another time and another place.

'No one else would use it?'

'Oh no, sir.' This time, thankfully, there was no corresponding curtsey, just a plain, clear answer.

Yellich examined the bristles of the brush and extracted one or two human hairs, short, dark looking, which he placed inside a second sachet. He emerged from the bathroom. 'What...' he asked Sally, 'no... How long did Mr Benjamin live here? There seems to be little of him in this room.'

'Of him, sir?'

'I mean...possessions, photographs...it's more like a hotel room than someone's bedroom in the family home.'

'Well, just a few months, sir.'

'I see. So where did he normally live?'

'In York, sir.'

'What did he do for a living? Was he married?'

Sally looked uncomfortable. 'I'm sorry, sir, but I am not to talk about the family with strangers. I have a position to keep, even if it's only for my husband's sake. Madam is very strict...we are not to talk about the family.'

'Is she?'

'Yes, sir.' Sally's voice trembled slightly.

'You're frightened of her?'

She nodded. 'Please don't ask me questions, sir.'

'I...we may have to and you will have to answer them. Do you know where Mr Benjamin is?'

'Please, sir...'

'That will do, Sally!' Annabella Tansey stood in the doorway of her son's bedroom. 'You did well.'

'Yes, ma'am.' Sally curtseyed and left the room.

'It is, as I said to you, Mr Yellich, the nature of the servant/employer relationship...you noted Sally's loyalty to me and the family. Woe betide her if she had answered questions which you should have put to me.'

Yellich paused. 'Let me make it plain to you, Mrs Tansey, I acknowledge that this is your home, I acknowledge your position as head of the household...'

'Thank you.'

'I also acknowledge that I am standing here with your permission...'

'Yes,' she nodded, 'I am pleased you understand that.'

'But...but...you must understand that the police will ask what questions they choose to ask and ask them of whom they choose to ask.'

Annabella Tansey flushed with anger. 'Have you obtained whatever it is you wish to obtain, Mr Yellich?'

'Yes...yes, I think I have.'

'Then there is no need to detain you any longer. I am sure

you are quite a busy man. You can see yourself out. Sally will be at her kitchen duties, preparing my lunch.'

'If the DNA of hair I have obtained from your son's bathroom doesn't match the DNA profile of the body that was found yesterday, we will not be returning...on this matter, anyway.'

'There is some other matter?'

'No...but none of us know what the future holds. On the other hand, if the DNA profile matches, we'll be returning.'

'Asking questions?' Said with an icy sneer.

'Yes...what we want to ask, and we will ask them of anybody we choose to ask.'

Annabella Tansey snorted with derision, turned on her heels and walked aggressively back to the upstairs sitting room, on the door of which servants must knock before being invited to enter.

Yellich, alone in Mister Benjamin's bedroom said, 'Good day to you, too.' He retraced his steps through the empty feeling, yet also hostile feeling, house to the front door. He stepped out of the shade of the house, into the heat of the sun, and walked to his car. He found he had not left a window wound down and so opened the door and stood a while, allowing the vehicle's interior to "breathe". As he stood there, he watched as Henry, the gardener wheeled the wheelbarrow towards the house, walking up the driveway. He smiled at Yellich and Yellich returned the smile.

'Afternoon, boss,' Henry said cheerily.

Yellich checked his watch, ten past noon. The morning had gone quickly. 'Afternoon,' he replied.

'Time for food,' Henry added, continuing to walk.

'Indeed...me too.'

'It's recycled.'

'What is?'

'The fountain water.' Henry spoke with a strong West

Indian accent. He was warm of personality and evidently didn't share his wife's timidity of Annabella Tansey. 'Folk get on a sweat 'bout all the water being wasted. Fact is, it's attached to a tank under the lawn, powered by an electric motor, same old water going round and round and round.' He stopped walking and put the wheelbarrow down when he was as close to Yellich as his route to the rear of the house was going to take him. 'Don't hardly lose any water, so no need to fret, boss...no need to fret. We have to top it up sometimes, but rain and snow melt does that mostly.'

'I see... I wasn't fretting, but I'm glad you told me. I feel happier knowing that...hate waste.'

'Yes, boss...and this is close on drought...ground's hard, as hard can be and no rain in the air, no rain at all.' He took his battered hat from his head and used it to wipe the sweat from his brow.

'You've a lot of ground to cover.'

'Too much, boss...there's twice as much at the back.'

'I saw. How much all told, do you know?'

'Five acres.'

'Five!'

'Not all garden. Missis owns the wood at the bottom of the back garden. There's about two acres for me to tend, but most of that is lawn. Plenty for me but not enough for two...just me and the garden all day, keeps me out of the house. Sally has a bad time in there. We're better off here.'

'You're not frightened of talking to strangers?'

'Depends what I say, boss...depends who I say it to.'

'I'm a police officer.'

'I know.'

'You know?' Yellich smiled.

'It's stamped on your forehead,' Henry smiled. 'I wasn't always a gardener. I was in the merchant navy when I was a young man...sailors have a girl in every port, but me...me, seemed like I had a cell in every port. It's the skin, you see. Get a little drunk, the white boys get sent back to their ship, the black fellas get a ride down town. It's the way the world turns. Anyway, I can recognise a cop fella when I see one.' Henry picked up the wheelbarrow and walked on.

Yellich watched him go and then sat in his car and started the engine. *Useful*, he thought as he drove slowly away, anxious to be seen to leave Sheringham on his terms should "m'lady" be watching him. If the DNA results match, and a return visit is necessary, then Henry, the gardener, might be a very useful "in", very useful indeed.

It was 12.20 hours.

Chapter Three

Monday, 14th of July, 09.00 – 14.05 hours
in which more information is gleaned about the murder victim and a house more modest than Sheringham is visited.

The Vale of York baked under a relentless sun. Black dogs and cats suffered. Only the tourists to the medieval city seemed to enjoy the heat, as if subscribing to the naïve belief that it had been provided for their holiday. Those who lived and worked in York and the Vale struggled doggedly, waiting for the sun to sink, hoping that the following day might bring with it a merciful drop in temperature or better still, a little rain, just a brief shower would so freshen things. That is the city of York, England, 54° north, 1° west of Greenwich. If it doesn't overheat in awful dryness in the summer, it floods in the winter when the Ouse rises and bursts its banks and the clergy of the Minster row a rowing boat up and back down the aisle, a great hoot for them but little comfort to the householders whose homes have been flooded, who have on occasion woken up to find three feet of water in their living room. York.

Hennessey leaned back in his chair while he held the report in one hand and a long glass of chilled soda water and lime in the other. 'Well, it's a confirmation.'

'Certainly is, boss.'

'Moves us forward. Tell me about the house.'

'Sheringham? Well, it's like going back in time, uncomfortably so...the plantation attitudes of the eighteenth and nineteenth centuries brought back across the Atlantic and planted in the famous and faire in the twenty-first century. Quite interesting in a way, not an enjoyable way, but nonetheless, interesting.'

'Like touching history?'

'Exactly, boss,' Yellich inclined his head. 'That's the phrase

I was looking for all last weekend…that's it, touching history.'

'Know what you mean, once saw a German woman interviewed who was young in the 1930s and 40s and who was a courtesan in a hotel in Bavaria established for the exclusive use of SS officers while on leave. I kid you not, she was an unreconstructed Nazi, what she said made my scalp crawl…but you suddenly realised you were back in the Nuremberg rallies. All other Nazis I have seen interviewed have been full of "I wasn't there and didn't know it was going on," or "it was my orders," but this female, forty, fifty years on was still convinced of the correctness of the Nazi cause…ugh,' Hennessey shuddered, 'but it was touching history and, as you say about Sheringham…interesting, but not in an enjoyable way.'

'Indeed.' Yellich sat back. He was dressed in light summer clothing. He had left his jacket hanging in his office, his shirtsleeves were rolled up. His back was saturated with sweat, causing his shirt to cling to it. He felt beads of sweat roll out of his scalp, down his forehead, down the nape of his neck.

'Didn't see a silver Mercedes in the drive way?'

'At Sheringham, sir? No, I didn't, no car in sight at all. Though large enough garage, as I recall.'

'Well, we'll find out, I dare say. So a new week, and fresh impetus into a case which has me intrigued.'

'Me too…headless and handless in the gorse.'

'Yes, I wrote it up on the file. Trip to Reed's farm was…was…of limited value. He was as described, "curmudgeonly", I think, is the word. He didn't notice a Mercedes-Benz in the lane or any car at all the day before the body was found. So if it was there, it was there only briefly.'

'Interesting point he made about townies though, I thought.'

'Yes…yes, it was. A countryman would have seen the significance of a cloud of flies above a mass of gorse in an instant, and so no countryman would even attempt to hide a body in gorse.' Hennessey paused. 'It's called "furze" in the south.'

'Gorse?'

'Yes. I first came across it on Blackheath Common when I was a nipper…jumped into it to retrieve a ball those – yellow flowers seemed so nice – and got badly cut on my legs. "That's furze," said my mother in that lovely East London accent she spoke with, "and that's what happens when you jump into furze."' He smiled. 'It's one of those new words I had to learn when I moved up here.'

'Furze,' Yellich repeated, committing a newly learned word to memory. 'I'll remember that.'

'Well, it will be useful if you're ever in London or south of, they'll look at you most quizzically if you talk about "gorse".'

'It's "furze" in the south, "gorse" in the north and "broom" in Scotland, I believe. Different name for the same animal.'

'Yes. So I think we visit Sheringham, tell Mrs Tansey the bad news and force a measure of co-operation from her.'

'Do we both need to see her, skipper?'

'Not really, no. What are you thinking, Yellich?'

'Well, sir, from my impression, as I have recorded, we'll get nothing from Sally, she's a frightened woman. I don't think Mrs Tansey will be forthcoming, even though her own son has been murdered. It'll be like drawing teeth, extracting information from her, but Henry, the gardener; he'll be more forthcoming. He's a man's man who doesn't get sufficient male company.'

'Being your impression?'

'Yes, boss, being my impression. He's been through the school of hard knocks and while he's not anxious to be deported back to Jamaica, equally he didn't seem to share his wife's terror of Mrs Tansey.'

'So you suggest?'

'Drop me at the gates, boss. Let me find Henry and engage him in conversation. See where I get.'

Hennessey smiled. 'Alright, I'll go and touch history by myself.'

Hennessey found Sally, Sheringham and Mrs Annabella Tansey, in that order, to be as Somerled Yellich had described. The first was fearful to the point of being mute; the second had an oppressive atmosphere; the third he found haughty, arrogant, disdainful, acidic. Hennessey, sitting on the settee as three days earlier Yellich had, observed Mrs Tansey, searching for some hint of emotion. He saw none.

'So he's gone and got himself killed? I did wonder. The possibility crossed my mind. He wasn't the body found in the woods?'

'Yes,' Hennessey spoke softly, 'yes, I am afraid he was.'

The room smelled heavily of furniture polish. An angry fly, unable to find any of the open windows, buzzed up and down the centre frame. Annabella Tansey turned her head and glared at it. 'Drat the thing,' she snapped, and then jabbed the bell in the wall beside her.

'I am afraid we have to ask some questions.'

'Not too personal, I hope?' She eyed Hennessey with the same piercing eyes Yellich had described. The lime green dress she had chosen to wear that day clashed with the red leather of the chair in which she sat, and glaringly so, in Hennessey's view.

'As close and personal as necessary, Mrs Tansey.'

'The newspapers said the body was headless?'

'It was.' Hennessey relaxed against the settee. 'I am sorry if that causes you distress.'

'Distress? The shame of it. Thank God his father isn't alive, it would destroy him.' She jabbed the bell again, fiercely, aggressively. 'Let himself get murdered...I can't believe that even of stupid Benjamin.' She paused, her jaw slackened, the piercing look in her eyes vanished to be replaced by a look of desperation. Hennessey smiled inwardly, pleased for her, the denial was lifting, now comes the acceptance, the realisation, the despair, the grief, all very healthy and then the unbridled determination to do whatever she could do to help the police apprehend her son's killer. *Now, now*, he thought, *now progress can be made.* But in the event she said, 'Who am I going to leave it all to now, now Benjy's gone? I was right...I was right...I was right...damn the man.'

There was a double knock at the door, just loud enough to be heard.

'Come!' Annabella Tansey shouted in response.

The door opened and timid Sally entered the room, made a slight curtsey and said timidly, 'You rang, ma'am?'

'Yes. Get rid of it.'

'Ma'am?'

'The fly...stupid girl, the fly.'

Sally walked to the window and as she did so, Hennessey said, 'Really, Mrs Tansey, it would have been no trouble for me.'

'Nonsense! You have guest status in this house, whether here officially or unofficially, you are a guest. Anyway, it's her job, it's what she gets paid for.'

Sally, having wafted the offending insect out of one of the open windows said, 'Will that be all, ma'am?'

'Yes.' That was all she said in reply. A curt "yes", nothing so courteous as a 'thank you'. Hennessey felt for Sally, life at Sheringham could not be easy for her. Sally exited the room silently, closing the door behind her with a soft 'click'.

'But I was right.'

'About what?'

'About having one child, one offspring. What good is one offspring, I said to my husband? There's no security in one child. We need at least three but he wouldn't have it...too noisy, too smelly. What did he say? "They smell of warm milk and vomit and make a noise totally disproportionate to their size." So one it was, especially because it was a boy...he could carry on the Tansey line...and that's another thing...this line of Tanseys has been unbroken for 400 years. Ha! I hope he turns in his grave. I said, "What if it's a girl? What if it's simple? What if it predeceases us and it's too late to have another?" I said all the "what ifs" I could think of but no, he had his wretched way. I even pointed out that I had to do all the hard work. I am led to believe that the male role in producing offspring is quite enjoyable. It's us, the weaker sex that have the hard work...but no...that didn't sway him. So Benjamin was born and that was the end of my reproductive life. But was I right?' She made a fist and beat the arm of her chair. 'Was I right? Was I right? Damn right, I was right.'

'Seems so, Mrs Tansey...but can we begin to look at Benjamin's life here in York and the Vale, especially in the last few months?'

'Yes. But I was right. Wasn't I right, Mr Hennessey, wasn't I right?'

'It would appear so.'

'Thank you. I am so pleased that someone agrees with me. So pleased.'

'Alright...now...a strange question, it might seem strange but it could possibly help us focus where we need to focus.'

'Yes.'

'A silver Mercedes-Benz.'

'Yes...'

'Do you own one such, or do you perhaps know of anyone who does?'

'No and no.'

'Alright.'

'I have a Rolls Royce.'

Hennessey went to say "of course" but checked himself and said, 'I see. Now, please tell me about your son, Benjamin.'

'What of him?'

Another fly flew in the open window, Mrs Tansey said, 'Damn,' and reached for the bell. Hennessey stood and said, 'Please...I insist,' and managed to save Sally another climb of the stairs to perform a function of little consequence. Once again seated, he said, 'Well, what was his address in York?'

'Oh...ugh! A pokey little slum within the walls. What is the name...one of Cromwell's generals?'

'Fairfax Street?'

'Yes, that's it. Number 103.'

Hennessey wrote the address in his notepad. One man's ceiling is another man's floor, he knew that, he had heard that observation before, but he felt that calling Fairfax Street a "slum" was unfair, even for the moneyed likes of Mrs Annabella Tansey. He knew the street; it was very near Micklegate Bar Police Station, two rows of terraced houses, neat, lovingly kept, sought after by the professional middle classes, separated from the wall by an elevated terrace of lawn, ideal for exercising small dogs or throwing frisbees – hardly a slum.

'Yes...little hut of a house. His wife lives there. I suppose there's about enough room for her if she doesn't complain too much.'

'His wife? Not his ex-wife?'

'No...wife. They're separated. Not yet fully divorced.'

'Ah...'

'Why? Is that a problem?'

'Strictly speaking, she's his next of kin.'

'Is she? Strictly speaking?'

'Yes. We'll have to inform her as soon as we can.'

'So you don't need my help?'

'Yes...yes, we do. We need help from everybody who knew Benjamin. We can continue talking, you are the reportee, she hasn't contacted us, probably because she doesn't know he's even missing. Unless…'

'There is no contact between me and that thing he married.'

'Alright. Her existence only became known to us during conversation with you, we can continue talking, but I will have to visit her immediately after leaving here. So…married. What was his occupation?'

'He occupied his business in great waters.'

'I am sorry?'

'He had a business involving small boats…pleasure craft, the things you see on the Ouse in summer. Those launches in Hull Marina…what's the term? "Gin palaces", never go anywhere, always stay tied up at the berth like floating caravans to the derision of yachtsmen who take their boats out in all weathers. My husband had a yacht in the Caribbean, what he used to say about "gin palaces" and the people who owned them, it would make even a police officer blush.'

Doubtful, thought Hennessey, *very doubtful*, but he knew what she meant. He asked, 'Do you know if he had enemies?'

'I don't, but I hope he did.'

'You hope he had enemies?'

'Yes, of course. It's my view that the measure of a man's success is not the number of friends he acquires, but in the number of enemies. I knew little of Benjamin's working life but I do so hope that he made enemies, lots and lots of lovely enemies, but the details, I know not.' She smiled. Presumably, thought Hennessey, at the thought of her son having made enemies, lots and lots of them. 'It would have pleased my husband…the thought that Benjamin would have made enemies in his business dealings. He was a disappointment to my husband, but if he had made enemies, my husband would have been pleased by that.'

'Your husband made enemies?'

'Oh, yes…he was ruthless. "All's fair in love and war," he

would say. Hardly original, I know, but he was fond of saying it. More than that, he lived it, it was his creed. He used to say, "Enemies in business means money in the bank."'

'I see. Benjamin never spoke to you about his business dealings, you say?'

'Yes, that's right. He sold boats, he had a brokerage…he wasn't a dealer in second-hand boats, nothing so lurid. He never actually owned the boats he sold, but he advertised them on behalf of their owners and brokered the sale with purchasers and took a commission…I believe that's how he earned his money.'

'Alright…now…outside his working life, what do you know of his social life?'

'Not a great deal.'

Silence. Annabella Tansey held eye contact with Hennessey.

'Well…' Hennessey shuffled in his seat, 'would you care to tell me what you do know?'

'He was married. He had a child.'

'A child?'

'William, ten years old.'

'Oh…' Hennessey groaned, 'I hadn't thought.'

'What? That a married man in his forties wouldn't have children?'

'No…not so much that, but more bad news to break. Not only does his wife not know he is deceased…but his son…old enough to understand. He will have to be told.'

'Do you want me to do it?'

'No!' Hennessey spoke quickly, alarmed at the thought of Annabella, Ice Maiden Tansey, breaking bad news to her daughter-in-law – the joy she would experience…'Thank you anyway, but it's something we should do, it's a job for the police and I would rather Mrs Tansey…'

'I am Mrs Tansey.'

'I meant your daughter-in-law.'

'I am still the only Mrs Tansey in this situation, my daughter-in-law, Sandra, refused to give up her maiden name upon marriage. It's a modern trend and I do detest it. She grew up as Sandra Cross and upon marrying continued to call herself Sandra Cross. Imagine how that made me feel...my son accepted it...my grandson is William Cross-Tansey. I didn't like her name coming before ours but I have to concede that if they were Tansey-Cross it would make them sound like mongrel dogs...so, small mercies, but I...I on the other hand was prepared – indeed honoured – to give up my maiden name, Semple, and take my husband's name in a gesture of commitment to my marriage...but girls today...'

'Well, I would rather Mrs Cross not be forewarned of our visit.'

'Why? Do you suspect her of having something to do with my son's murder?'

'Yes.'

'You do?'

'Yes...yes, because at this stage everybody is suspect.'

'Everybody? Including me?'

'Everybody...everybody has the finger of suspicion pointed at them. Over the next few days or weeks the finger of suspicion will be lifted from one or two, and so on...until only the culprit remains. It is the way most crimes are solved.'

'You hope. Because we both know some murders are never solved.'

Hennessey inclined his head in acknowledgement of the accuracy of Mrs Tansey's statement. 'But most are...even if it takes years to obtain a conviction, most murders are solved and by most, I don't mean fifty-one per cent, I mean ninety per cent plus.' Hennessey paused. 'Benjamin was living here when he died. Presumably he was still working?'

'Yes...right up until he left here for the last time.'

'When was that, Mrs Tansey?'

'Monday.'

'Morning?'

Mrs Tansey looked uncomfortable. 'I presume so.'

'Only presume?'

'Well, he was here on Sunday evening...he wasn't here on Monday when I woke...ask Sally, she'll tell you.'

'I think I will.'

Mrs Tansey seemed to Hennessey to stiffen. He sensed he was nudging an uncomfortable area. 'Is there something you want to tell me, Mrs Tansey? Is there something I should know?'

'No...to both questions.' Hennessey thought she said it with too much finality to be truthful. *Something*, he thought, *something is here hid*. He said, 'I'd like to see your son's bedroom.'

Yellich enjoyed Henry's company. The man, late middle-aged, proved himself to be a man with a ready smile and a warmth in his eyes. They sat together on a log, hidden from view from Sheringham by dense shrubbery.

'It's my little hideaway.' Henry filled a pipe with dark tobacco. 'You don't have a pipe, law fella?'

'No,' Yellich smiled as he shook his head, 'no vices.'

'Not even the drink?'

'Not even the drink.'

'Teetotal?'

'No...no...not teetotal...but a long way from going to the pub each night.'

'You have a family?'

'Wife, one son.'

'Just one?'

'Just one.'

'Plan more...you're still young, law fella.'

'No…no plans for any more.'

'Knew you'd come back.'

'Oh…?'

'Yes, I know. I told you, I know lawmen. I saw that look in your eye. I saw the way you looked…said I, "Yon law fella will be back," and here you are.'

'Just the look, or did you…do you, know something?'

'Hey, man,' Henry plunged a meaty paw into his shirt pocket and took out a box of matches. He struck one and laid the flame across the bowl of his pipe, sucking air through the stem as he did so. He took the pipe out of his mouth and blew out the match flame and tossed the spent match onto an area of tilled soil. 'Man, I know lots of things, but whether they're what the law wants to know…well, I don't know.'

'Okay, Henry, so what do you know about Benjamin Tansey?'

'Mr Benjamin?' He drew lovingly on the pipe. 'Well, not a happy man. Not a happy man at all.'

'Oh?'

'Never measured up, just not up to his parents' mark…never good enough. Seemed alright to me, never messed up, got qualifications…got married…had children. I'd be happy if any son of mine did that, but the Tanseys…if you gave them perfection, they'd pick fault with it.'

'He got divorced?'

'You asking me, law fella?'

'Just want to know why he was living here.' Yellich brushed a fly away from his face.

'Okay. Yes, he got divorced. Or separated. Marriage failed anyway.'

'When did he come back to Sheringham?'

'Crocus time.'

'March, April?'

'Yes…'bout that time. Nice time of the year,

springtime...newness, everything is fresh, life goes on. Went to a funeral once...I mean one funeral I attended, walked home, a late snow on the ground and the crocuses were pushing up through the snow...*life goes on*, I thought, *bury one old boy and look but here's newness...all in the same day*. Like autumn the best...been in England too long.'

'You think so?'

'Yeah...I'm from Jamaica, man, now I am thinking the English summer is too hot. When that happens to any West Indian who isn't born here, that means they've been here long enough, time to go home. You know, in Jamaica...in the West Indies all over...we say you die eighteen inches up,' he tapped his knee, 'from here up. So your feet remain alive to walk your body home.'

Yellich smiled. 'Really?'

'Yes, cop man, really. The English summers are getting too hot for old Henry; time for Henry and girl Sally to be making tracks. We don't want to die in England.'

'You've years in you yet, Henry.' Yellich took his notebook from his pocket. 'Just for our records, you are Mr and Mrs...?'

'Chambers. Way back a plantation owner of that name would have kept slaves. My ancestors would have taken his name when they were freed up.'

'Chambers,' Yellich echoed as he wrote. 'Well at least you know the origin of your name, mine's Yellich. We think it's Eastern European, modified by the British influence, like some immigration official who couldn't manage the original, the closest he could get was "Yellich". Mind you, that's better than being named after your jewellery, which is how folk called Ruby or Diamond acquired their surnames.'

Henry Chambers laughed. 'Never knew that.'

'Well...were you close enough to Benjamin to find out who would want to murder him?'

'No, can't tell you that, never that close. Can tell Mrs

Tansey's hurting inside, don't let that rock hard exterior fool you. She's hurting alright.'

'I confess I did wonder. I mean a mother...her only child...'

'It's an act. She doesn't think she should show weakness but my girl Sally, she heard her over the weekend wailing for the man-child when she thought no one was around. I am not so frightened of her as my girl Sally but then I'm out here all the livelong day, suits my fancy, but I've been her gardener now for a long time and I see things...over the years I see things and you listen when old Henry tells you she's hurting, because she is.'

'That's interesting to know.'

'Tell you something else, you said "her only child".'

'Yes.'

'Ain't so.'

'No?'

'Well, secrets are like these plants...these plants here, you can bury them but they won't stay hidden...not for ever...like the crocuses in the spring, they'll pop out of the ground, and even through snow...all brightly coloured and that's them only just begun to grow.'

'So, more children?'

'One more...another male. Anything that happens in the house, my girl Sally will tell me...after a while, sometimes years. My girl Sally's head, it's like a seedbed, things get planted but they'll grow after a while. So one day, Sally tells me that Benjamin is feeling the edge of his mother's tongue and she said – Mrs Tansey, that is – she said, "I should have kept the first one and got rid of you".'

'Oh...'

'Not a good thing to say to anyone, especially your son.'

'Sally overheard that?'

'Sally was in the room polishing the silver, so far as ma'am was concerned, she wasn't there at all…servants don't have ears, so you can say what you like in front of them and only talk to them when you want something.'

'She had a pregnancy terminated? "Got rid of it," is that what she meant?'

Henry Chambers shook his head. 'No…don't think she meant that. My girl Sally said that ma'am then said, "I don't know what he's doing now, but it will be something and I mean *something*." So had him taken care of…given to the nuns, whatever you do with unwanted children.'

'When was that said?'

'Not too long ago. After the master died, when Madam was a widow woman, my girl Sally…you know women have an intuition that we don't have.'

'You think so?'

'I know so.' Henry Chambers turned to Yellich and smiled a warm, fatherly, if not grandfatherly, smile. "Listen to my words of wisdom, my dear good boy," that sort of smile. 'Believe me, I know so. Anyway, my girl Sally thought that Mrs Tansey…widow Tansey by then, was letting something out, something she had kept bottled up inside her all the live-long days of her marriage. Somewhere out there was a lovechild of an earlier encounter.' Henry Chambers pulled on his pipe. 'Managed to keep it from him. I mean, a man knows if a woman has given birth, you must know that, being a father.'

'Yes.'

'But we don't know what goes on in our neighbours' bed-chamber, that's the old way of the world, wouldn't want it any other way.'

'Me neither. Ever see a silver Mercedes-Benz about Sheringham?'

'No.' Said with definite confidence. 'Wouldn't know what a Mercedes-Benz is. I know it's a car, but I have never seen a silver car in Sheringham. So no silver Mercedes, not while I have been tending these grounds summer and winter, year in, year out...and I helped Mrs Tansey move in. So, no silver Mercedes at all, ever. I would have seen it. Sure I would have seen it.'

The man came down the stairs of his house from his bedroom and opened the kitchen door. He stopped as if suddenly frozen.

It had happened again.

Occasionally, and not infrequently, somebody had done something for him. Just come into his house and done something...and had left...just gone away, stole away into the night.

This time it was the kitchen. Usually untidy...now, that morning, it was clean and neat.

She was slender of figure and also slender of face with black hair that, centre parted, fell smoothly to either side of her head to her shoulders. She was about five foot two inches tall, he thought. She wore a pale grey blouse over a knee length cream coloured skirt which was held up by a thin black leather belt. Bare legs finished in pale coloured shoes, with just a hint of a heel. Very feminine, not plain, but not meretricious either, thought Hennessey, a woman who was happy with herself, happy to be herself. She sat back on the settee in her house on Fairfax Street, absorbing the news. She needed time, she needed space. Hennessey and Yellich allowed her such, and used the time to read the room.

It was, not surprisingly to either officer, cramped in comparison to Sheringham. Hennessey fancied that if the bottom of Sandra Cross's house was the floor of the room in which they at present sat, and the top was the ceiling of the bedroom, which would doubtless be above, then this entire house

could, end on end, fit three times into the room in which
Annabella Tansey had received Yellich, and later Hennessey.
The room seemed, to Hennessey, to be tastefully decorated; a
floor covering of hardwearing matting, prints of great paintings on the wall though, pleasingly, nothing trite or "chocolate
box top". The prints, one either side of and above the mantelpiece, were of works by lesser-known artists and showed a
Victorian rural landscape. Both seemed to speak of cold
weather and of relentless labour, though the brushwork in
both Hennessey thought to be masterful. A third painting
hung above the settee on which a pale looking Sandra Cross
sat, as if deflated. It too showed a Victorian scene but was an
urban, rather than rural, landscape, though it too spoke of
cold and poverty and hardship. A pile of magazines with a pair
of reading glasses on them lay on a low table. A sheepskin rug
lay on the floor in front of the fire. The wallpaper was of a
gentle blue and the curtains a plain but darker shade of blue.

'Well, now she'll have to decide whether she is going to
keep her word.'

'Who?'

'The She-Devil of Sheringham.' Sandra Cross forced a
smile as she wiped a tear from her eye.

'What word is that?'

'That she will not allow a penny of her fortune to go to me
or William, unless I relinquish my name and call myself Mrs
Tansey and have William's name changed from Cross-Tansey
to plain Tansey. While Benjamin was alive, she knew she had
someone to leave it to. Now she's going to have to think.
Mind you, the answer's plain.'

'It is?'

'Of course it is. All she need do is leave it in trust for
William upon his reaching a certain age when he is young
enough to enjoy the money but old enough to value it,
say...thirty years...conditional upon his relinquishing his

double-barrelled name, and becoming a Tansey. Mind you, she's probably already done that, she's a shrewd old bat, she looks after her own. Her maid's had a hip replacement, at her expense. I mean at Mrs Tansey's expense. She treats them like slaves, but when Sally's hip seized up, no waiting for three years to get it done on the National Health, not a chance. It was done privately within a week or two. She said she did it because she couldn't abide a maid limping about Sheringham, but that was her refusing to accept that she was looking after her own. Had to keep up the "hard woman of the manor" image. But it will be interesting to see what she says about leaving money to William now.' She glanced out of the window, the view was of Fairfax Street, parked cars, the houses opposite.

'He's out playing with friends?'

'Yes.' Sandra Cross shook her head. It's going to be difficult...telling him...he loves his father...at the moment he loves him, as from tomorrow, he will have loved him. I read the story in the paper, the headless body. I never...never thought it could be Benjamin...but murdered?'

'Well, we have to assume murder.'

'What else could it be?'

'People have disposed of bodies after they have been killed accidentally...but...the decapitation and the removal of the hands, it seems to point to murder.'

'But who would want to do that to Benjy?'

'We don't know.' Hennessey spoke softly.

'That's why we are here,' Yellich added, equally softly. 'Supposing you tell us?'

Sandra Cross looked at Yellich, then Hennessey, then at Yellich. 'I don't know.' She spoke with a noticeable trace of alarm. 'You mustn't think...'

'Mrs Cross,' Hennessey spoke firmly, 'please don't tell us what we must not think...this is a murder investigation and we will think what we will think. So please allow us to ask questions. I gather you and your husband were separated?'

'Yes,' she looked uncomfortable. 'There's no secret there, but I am embarrassed by it. What woman isn't embarrassed when her marriage fails?'

'That really depends on why it failed.'

'Well, even if he deserted, you'd think why was it that I couldn't keep him? Not clever enough...not young enough anymore?'

'So, he left you?'

'Yes.'

'Did he give any reason?'

'None. He packed his bags and went home to the She-Devil.'

'Who is probably not all bad. I have heard the animals with the hardest shells have the softest centres.'

'Yes,' Sandra Cross nodded in agreement. 'Yes, I have heard that expression.'

'And in my years as a police officer, I have met many a soft spoken, mild mannered person who could kill without compulsion and smile as he or she did so.'

'What's that supposed to mean!' Sandra Cross shot a cold glare at Hennessey. 'Am I under suspicion?'

'Yes.'

Her head sagged, she held her forehead, 'It's bad enough you came to tell me I am a widow, and to leave me to tell my son he's fatherless, now I am accused of murder...this is too much.'

'I am sorry, but we have a job to do and in such circumstances we have an expression, "Before you look at the outlaws, look at the in-laws."'

She raised her eyebrows, 'That's not very funny.'

'It's not supposed to be,' Hennessey said.

'It's accurate,' Yellich added. 'There are six chances in ten that any given murder victim will be murdered by someone close to them, three in ten by someone remote but also known to them in some capacity and one in ten that they will have been murdered by a total stranger.'

'Do you have an alibi for Monday evening, last Monday evening?'

'A week ago today? I don't know, I don't keep a diary…at home I suppose, just me and William.'

'You don't work?'

She shook her head. 'Just get an allowance from Benjamin, but it doesn't go far.'

'I see. So why did you and your husband separate?'

'What relevance is that?'

'We don't know if it is until you tell us.'

'No one reason…things accumulated. Benjamin said, "I think we should separate," and I said, "That's a good idea." It was a bit more heated than that but that was the gist of it. Anyway, he packed his bags and drove to Sheringham.'

'You saw him after that?'

'Oh yes, weekly. He came to visit William, take him out…took him to watch York City when it was the football season…took him fishing.' She began to fight back tears.

'What are your finances like?'

'Tight. Couldn't be tighter. It looks comfortable but if I need something for the house, I go to the charity shops…my clothes come from there…the shoes are new though.' She forced a smile. 'The food…well, there's a trough in the supermarket where they throw all the feed that's reached its sell-by date. I dive into it on a nearly daily basis…so…tight, couldn't get much tighter.'

'And you've just explained, you wouldn't benefit from your husband's death, financially speaking?'

'From her? No. William might…I won't. I'm proud of my name…I am not giving it up.'

'Is the house yours?'

'Yes…well, it's mortgaged, not rented…mind you, it will be mine outright soon.'

'Oh?'

'You can prove the body is that of Benjamin?'

'Yes,' Hennessey said simply, calmly. 'There is no equivocation.'

Sandra Cross nodded with pursed lips. 'Then there will be a death certificate?'

'Yes.'

'Then, in that case, the insurance company will pay out on Benjamin's death, and the house will be mine. We opted for a simple repayment, plus a life insurance for the value of the house. The company will pay out because his death can be proven and then this little house will be mine and the William's.'

'So you wouldn't benefit from his death, I mean, financially speaking?'

'As I told you, I am too pigheaded to give up my surname. Expensive decision you might think.' She shrugged her shoulders.

'It is, rather.' Hennessey admired her principles. 'Now, can I ask if you know of anyone who might want to harm your husband?'

'Harm him?' Sandra Cross smiled at Hennessey. 'That's a rather delicate way of phrasing the inevitable question. You mean who'd want to kill him, don't you?'

'Yes…if you like.'

'Well, let's be direct about it. It is in both our interests.'

'Indeed.'

'Well, the answer is, no, I don't. Benjamin and I are estranged…we are…we were heading for divorce at a rate of knots, like about Mach 3, so he wasn't standing in my way in respect of any involvement I might be having with A.N. Other.'

'Are you seeing someone?'

She looked at him with a raised eyebrow. 'Is that relevant? Is that any of your concern?'

'It might be relevant and so yes, it is our concern.'

'No, I'm not.' She turned her head away. 'Benjamin and I didn't separate because of any infidelity...on either side. The marriage just wasn't working, plain as that. We had stopped being an item...we had stopped thinking the same way. I dare say other couples wouldn't have seen that as a reason to throw in the towel, but we are not other couples, we are – we were Mr and Mrs Cross-Tansey of Fairfax Street, York, and the only thing that we did think alike about was that our own personal fulfilment could not be achieved if we remained together. So we separated. Amicably.'

'Amicably?'

'Yes...no really big rows...no launching furniture at each other while the children cowered beneath the tables or up in their rooms. All very calm and businesslike and, what's more, contrary to what folk say, William benefited.'

'He did?'

'Yes...behaviour and schoolwork both improved, considerably so. He had lived in an increasingly stressed household until then, you see, and it told on him. We didn't realise how much he was affected by our marriage going pear-shaped. So when you hear of couples staying together for the sake of the children, well, it's not always the right thing to do. Our experience was that separating has been the best thing for William, but that is a long-winded way of saying that there was no lover driven to murder Benjamin out of jealousy for me. Quite frankly, I couldn't cope with the demands of a relationship and William, and now I have to find work. I wouldn't be able to live on what the state will allow me...so even less time for a boyfriend. William wouldn't be able to cope with one either, it'll be too soon after losing his father. Oh heavens,' she ran her hand through her hair. 'What time is it?'

Hennessey and Yellich both glanced at their watches, but only Hennessey spoke. 'Approaching midday.'

'He'll be home for his lunch soon. He's out with his friends…school holidays…roll on September. Will you gentlemen be long? I'd rather they not see you. I'd rather have the house to myself when I have to tell him about Benjamin.'

Hennessey glanced at Yellich, then turned to Mrs Cross. 'Not long, though we might…in fact, certainly will, be calling again.'

'Yes…yes. I imagine you will.'

'So nothing…nobody in Mr Tansey's private life to explain his murder? What about his working life? He was a businessman, businessmen make enemies?'

'I know little of his affairs, in fact I know nothing. I know where his office is, he has a partner and a secretary, and that's all I know.'

'Where are the premises?'

'Stuck up a snickelway in the centre of York: 27 Mad Alice Lane.'

'Not a large concern then?'

'No, but he doesn't need a large concern; he's a broker, he sells boats. He matches purchasers with sellers, brokers the deal and takes a commission on the sale. He also brokers marine insurance and takes a commission for each policy he sells. Not a great big honey pot as our little house might tell you. The people on this street are what I believe are called "lower professionals": teachers, probation officers, middle-ranking managers, and we live side by side with them and our lifestyle gels with our neighbours…so not a money spinning operation. We don't live with the doctors, lawyers and accountants.'

'It is, nonetheless, a very comfortable house.'

'Thank you,' she forced a smile, 'I am not unhappy here,

probably just as well now. Unless I win the lottery, which I won't because I don't do it, it looks like I'll be here for some time to come, you'll always know where to find me.' She patted the arm of the settee. 'Widowhood,' she said softly. 'Like every married woman, I have learned to live with the prospect of becoming a widow. I just didn't expect it so soon…and not in these circumstances…I mean murder.'

'Yes…the nature of the post-mortem injuries.'

'Delicate again…you mean that his head was chopped off.'

'Yes…again…if you like.'

'Well, my father was a miner, my brothers were pitmen at the Wistow Colliery, I grew up in a blunt spoken family.'

'Calling a spade a spade?'

'Call a spade a bloody shovel, more like. So, his head was chopped off, but that was after he was dead?'

'Yes…definitely.'

She nodded a "thank you". 'Well, that's something. I read an article about beheading once. Whether it be by axe or guillotine, it is neither instantaneous nor painless, the brain remains alive for some minutes after decapitation and the person can be conscious. The mouth makes no sound because the vocal chords are severed, but that doesn't mean the person is not in great pain.'

'Yes,' Hennessey said, 'I have read the same. In fact I read once that following her decapitation, the lips of Mary Queen of Scots were observed to move as if in prayer for fifteen minutes.'

'As long as that?' Sally Cross again raised an eyebrow. 'Blimey, I thought three or four minutes, and that is long enough to know that your head has been severed from your body. But Benjy was definitely dead before this?'

'Yes.'

'How do you know, may I ask?'

'Yes, you may ask. The pathologist…she…'

'She? A lady pathologist?'

'Yes, Dr D'Acre. She is very thorough, we are lucky to have her. Well, she observed that your husband's blood was still in his body, albeit in a congealed state. It showed her that the head and the hands were removed between twenty-four and forty-eight hours after he died. If he had been decapitated whilst alive, his blood would have flowed out of the venous and jugular arteries at the neck.'

'I see. There is some comfort there. Do you know how he died?'

'We don't. There were no injuries to the body, so we have to presume he died of head injuries.'

'Oh Benjy...Benjy.' Sandra Cross once again seemed to be fighting back tears. 'Please, if that's all.' She stood slowly, gracefully. 'I would like some time to compose myself before William returns. I still don't know what I am going to say to him.'

'Of course.' Hennessey also stood, Yellich did likewise. 'Just one more question.'

'Yes?'

'Do you know of anyone, also known to your late husband, who owns a silver Mercedes-Benz?'

'What?' She shook her head. 'A silver Mercedes,' she forced a laugh, 'in Fairfax Street? No...no, I don't.'

'Alright.' Hennessey smiled, but he noted a look of alarm in Sally Cross's eyes at the mention of the car, its colour and make, a look which she couldn't conceal.

Yellich and Hennessey walked the short distance back to Micklegate Bar Police Station. They signed in at the enquiry desk and stood side by side, silently checking the content of their pigeonholes. Both officers had received nothing other than routine circulars, one of which was the hardy perennial, requesting and reminding staff, where possible, to use second-class postage and make phone calls after 2.00pm, when the call rate is reduced. It also requested staff to write on both sides of a sheet of paper, again, wherever possible. The memo was circulated every six months and both officers, recognising it, and being able to recite it word for word, screwed it up and tossed it into the wastepaper bin that stood beneath the pigeonholes and was, by then, already full of read, digested and discarded memos.

'Lunch?' Hennessey turned to Yellich.

'Canteen for me, skipper.'

Hennessey smiled. 'Don't know how you can stand that gruel.'

'My wallet likes it well, boss.'

'Yes, that can be the only reason. Well, shall we say my office at 2.00pm? Review the morning's work?'

'Very good, sir, 2.00pm.'

Hennessey signed out and left the red brick police station which glowed in the sun as only northern red brick can glow, giving the impression to any observer standing in excess of a hundred metres away that the building was aflame, and crossed the road and took the steps up the wall at Micklegate Bar. He turned left and walked the section of wall from the Bar to Lendal Bridge, knowing, as any citizen of York knows, that walking the walls is by far the speediest way to cross the medieval centre of the ancient city. The walls on that day were crowded with tourists and locals weaving in and out of each other and it convinced Hennessey, as a crowded wall always managed to do, that the City Fathers should introduce a one-way system of travel along the walls, there being nothing on the inside of the wall to prevent someone from falling six feet onto a steeply inclined grass bank. Such a fall, he conceded, was highly unlikely to prove fatal, but it could easily cause fractures in the limbs of frail, elderly persons. Yet the accident waiting to happen, never seemed to occur, even on crowded walls. He had lived in the city for the greater part of his adult life, yet he had never seen, heard or even read of an incident wherein a person fell off the inside edge of the wall. Nonetheless, he walked as he always tried to walk, next to the battlements on the outside edge, leaving the inside edge to excited youths and school parties who seemed not to recognise the danger. He left the wall at Lendal Bridge, as indeed he was obliged to – York's walls being incomplete and existing only in three remaining sections of the original, fully encircling wall – and crossed the Ouse by Lendal bridge. He glanced to his left as he crossed the bridge where the girls used to stand before being pressured by the authorities to move their trade indoors, into massage parlours, or taking the half hour fast train to Leeds to stand behind the Corn Exchange or on the legendary Spencer Place in Chapeltown which, Hennessey found, was, despite its name, a thoroughfare. The Ouse, at midday in high summer, gave off a blue hue and looked invitingly cool. A tall, wide-based pleasure cruiser was tied to the bank as passengers boarded, many with children, for a cruise on the river, and smaller motorboats suitable for four persons only "phutted" by, each identical to the other, and hired by the hour from the wharf close to the Lower Skeldergate Bridge. A blonde-haired girl pulled a single scull with ease and confidence. On the road to his left, a motor vehicle with trailers, which evoked a steam locomotive with coaches, carried tourists to the National Railway Museum, from which the shrill whistle of a "steamie" would occasionally be heard. Two well-groomed mares pulled a polished open coach. The measured tread of their hooves Hennessey found particularly comforting and reassuring. Open topped buses with a recorded commentary, doing the York tour, shared the crowded road space with other buses on normal services, and also with motorcars whose drivers were clearly unversed with the city on a summer's day and had blundered into a mistake they wouldn't make again, or were foolish enough to believe they would enjoy a smooth transit, despite the crowds. Hennessey turned off Museum Street, on which Lendal Bridge stood, and into Lendal itself. He walked on the left-hand side of the road which, whilst not pedestrianised, was occupied more by pedestrians than it was by motor vehicles, past the imposing Judges' Residence, past small shops, each doing a thriving trade, past revolving postcard stands standing on the pavement, past small restaurants from which music spilled out of open windows. In St Helen's Square, more tourists milled as buskers, some more skilled than others, entertained for passing coins. The man who sang loudly to a few limited guitar chords had, Hennessey observed, significantly less coins in his collection cap than the two young women, dressed in cheesecloth shirts and ankle length cotton skirts, who gave a polished violin duo performance. The music of the latter, Hennessey felt to be sweet beyond sweetness, of surpassing melodiousness. He felt his soul elevated and, as he passed, he was moved to drop a two-pound coin into the upturned bowler hat that lay at their feet. He received a nod and a smile of thanks from one of the girls and as he did so, he looked into the girl's sparkling eyes and saw a personality which, while not perhaps naïve, seemed thus far to have escaped hurt by life's cruelty and unfairness and inhumanity. She was, he thought, a very fortunate young woman, matured from childhood to be pleasing of face and figure and also to have, to date, escaped the great wrath that can be the human experience.

Hennessey dined at a small Italian restaurant, a modest lunch of lasagne, and seemed to both surprise and disappoint the waiter by not ordering wine, but insisting rather on mineral water. He returned to Micklegate Bar Police Station with a sense of well being that only a pleasing meal can provide. At 2.00pm he was seated at his desk. At one minute past two he was joined by Somerled Yellich.

The man contrived to walk down Fairfax Street at a time when he thought there might be a good chance of encountering the boy. Indeed, they passed each other close to the boy's house. The boy looked pale, as if he had been crying...there was a lost and confused look about him. The man smiled warmly and said, 'Hello there'. The boy tried to smile in return, and the man could tell that his warmth was appreciated. *It's all about grooming*, he thought as he walked on. *Careful, careful grooming...and needy children.*

Chapter Four

Monday, 21st of July, 14.30 – 23.00 hours
*in which an earlier murder assumes a new significance and
George Hennessey is at home to the gentle reader.*

The man was nervous. That was plain. He sat as if frozen,
leaning slightly forward, trying to smile but continually pulled
the fingers of his left-hand with his right, one by one, until
they clicked in their sockets, and would then use his left-hand
to pull at the fingers of his right hand, then would swap hands
and the process would continue, all the while smiling a very
false, I-am-trying-to-please-you smile. The man was in his
thirties, had blonde, collar length hair, piercing green eyes. He
wore a grey suit, white shirt, red tie, occasionally an expensive
looking watch would protrude from under the cuff of his left
wrist, especially when he was wrenching at the fingers of his
right-hand. The office in Mad Alice Lane was, as Sandra Cross
had described it, small. Really it was just two rooms, one
above the other; a small room at ground level occupied by a
secretary who smiled at Hennessey and Yellich, as if assuming
they were customers with money to part with, but whose attitude cooled when they showed their IDs. A door at the side
of the secretary's desk indicated the presence of a small utili-
ty room allowing for basic human needs to be answered during the working day. Framed photographs of expensive looking pleasure craft, both sail and power, hung on the wall, and
a rubber plant stood next to the narrow, very narrow, stairway
that Hennessey and Yellich were invited to ascend in order to
speak to Mr Scaife. Scaife opened the door of his office upon
the police officer's knock and he too welcomed them warmly
until Hennessey and Yellich identified themselves, at which he
sat behind his desk, appeared to assume a rigid, sitting position
and disconcertingly, but to the officers, very interestingly,

began to pull at his fingers, one after the other. His room was also cramped, low beams, a window which looked down into the snickelway that was Mad Alice Lane, off Lower Petergate. So named Hennessey had once read, after the lady who once lived there and, in 1825, was executed at York Castle for the unpardonable sin of being insane. Lund's Court was, he had noted, an official alternative, but less colourful name for what was one of the more pleasant snickelways of old York, having room for a small courtyard along its length as it twisted between ancient buildings and under low roofs from Low Petergate to Swinegate, and thus providing a magical walk of about 150 feet. Scaife's room was also adorned with framed photographs of boats, the sort of boats that are rich men's toys. His desktop was neat, uncluttered, and a pale blue filing cabinet stood beside the desk. A door was set in the wall beside the filing cabinets. In front of the desk were two chairs, black leather on stainless steel frames. When invited to do so, Hennessey sat in one, Yellich in the other.

'You are?'

'Scaife…Robert Scaife.'

'Mr Tansey's business partner?'

'Oh, I wish…I wish. No, I am his office manager, he employs me.' The smile was fixed in place as his body posture, the wrenching of the fingers, continued.

'I see.' Hennessey glanced around him. 'Where does Mr Tansey work?'

'In there.' Scaife indicated the door to his right. 'These ancient buildings…a rabbit warren.'

'Yes, I know.'

'We took over this property five years ago. Benjamin…Mr Tansey, decided to strip it right back. His business is modern boats but his passion was for ancient buildings. Heavens…what did we find? Ancient coins, not particularly valuable but Mr Tansey saved them, a pistol…'

'A pistol!'

'Yes, an ancient flintlock, in reasonable condition, we found it under a loose floorboard. We donated that to the museum. The house…the building, dates from the fourteenth century we believe, so it's seen some history.'

Very eager to tell us anything at all, Hennessey thought, like schoolchildren who attempt to frustrate their teacher's class by encouraging him or her to talk about his or her favourite subject, whatever that may be, so long as it isn't French or Maths or Science. 'Well,' he said, 'you'll gather that we are here to talk about Mr Tansey…interesting as the building may be.'

'Yes, it came as quite a shock…decapitated. Who'd do that?'

'Indeed,' Hennessey smiled. 'One nail struck very firmly on the head, Mr Scaife, very firmly indeed.'

'Yes.'

'It is the "who" of it which drives our investigation.'

Scaife shrugged. 'I wish I could help you. I have no idea who would…who could do such a thing.'

'Perhaps you might know who would want to? The "why" is often the route to the "who".'

'The motive, you mean?'

'Yes, Mr Scaife. I mean the motive. Do you know of anyone who would want to murder Mr Tansey or anyone who has a silver Mercedes-Benz?'

'No.' Scaife shook his head vigorously, too vigorously to be sincere in Hennessey's view. Beside him he felt Yellich stiffen with growing suspicion. 'No, I don't. Benjy, Mr Tansey, was well liked. I have worked for him for seven…eight years. Geraldine, below…our secretary, she has been with us since we moved into these premises and was prepared to get dirty. She put her overalls on and scraped and scrubbed. Not many young girls, fearful of breaking their fingernails, would do that. But that was Benjamin; he inspired that sort of loyalty and five years, that's a long time for a secretary to stay with a firm. Secretaries move about like they are playing musical chairs. So Geraldine has been very loyal to us. I fear now though, well, I think she'll be moving on, as indeed I possibly will. We may well both have to.'

'Oh?'

'Well, we are both employees, our employer is deceased…a small firm…we are both redundant. Geraldine has work to keep her busy, I…well, I have nothing to do but sit here and think about my future, and I confess it looks a trifle bleak. I doubt that Mrs Cross – that's Benjamin's wife…her name…'

'Yes,' Hennessey held up his hand, 'thank you, we know the story of the name.'

'Silly, pigheaded female,' Scaife shook his head in a gesture of despair. 'What's wrong with changing your name upon marriage? Women have done it for centuries, and the fortune she could have had. Have you seen Sheringham?'

'Yes, we know about the fortune in Mr Tansey's family.'

'Well, I don't know Mrs Cross well, but I doubt she will be interested in taking over. I can see only one of two paths ahead of me; another job with another company, or taking over here. I was pondering that before you came. If Mrs Cross will sell to me…I could steal his customers.'

'Steal?' Hennessey's ears pricked up. 'What do you mean?'

'Well, I don't mean "steal" in the criminal sense.' Scaife corrected himself, continuing to speak in a nervous manner. 'You see, I could set up on my own, take over the rental of this property, write to all our customers and tell them of the unfortunate death of Benjamin and invite them to allow me to continue to act for them. But an established name means a lot in any business and it took me and Benjamin ten years' hard work to establish the good name of Tansey Marine Brokers. I really haven't the energy to start again and work for another ten years to establish the good name of Scaife Marine Brokers. I'd really like to buy the firm. I think Mrs Cross will sell. It may seem like a lazy way of doing it, but it's attractive to me.' He glanced at the filing cabinet beside him. 'There's five hundred boats on our books…didn't know you could get five hundred boats in a filing cabinet, did you?' He smiled at the joke. 'It's actually one of Benjy's jokes,' he said apologetically when he saw that Hennessey and Yellich were determined to remain stone-faced. 'He would amuse the customers with it, "It's easy," he would say, "one hundred and twenty-five in each drawer." Suppose it wasn't particularly funny but it was a useful icebreaker if a customer was new to boating and was pondering parting with a lot of money. We have one boat on our books, its asking price is a quarter of a million quid and that's at rock bottom knockdown. She's lying in the Balearics. If we…if I…can find a buyer, we get ten percent of that sale, that's more than some people earn in a year. Then there is the insurance to broker, add another five thousand in commission for that, and you see how the business works.'

'Yes, nice line of work.'

'Well, it could be if we had more boats like that on our books, but unfortunately, we don't, most of our customers are at the lower end of the market, and there's a recession; people are not buying boats at the moment. Hence Benjamin and Sandra's little house in Fairfax Street.'

'I see.' Hennessey shuffled in his seat. 'So you'll be contacting Mrs Cross?'

'Yes, when it's more appropriate. I'll go round and make overtures along business lines. At the moment, well, things are up in the air…grieving widow, bereaved child, funeral to arrange. I'll keep the business ticking over…hardly onerous…you can see how furiously the phones are ringing…then in a couple of weeks I'll walk to Fairfax Street, it's not far from here, and after the niceties, offer a fair price.'

'Is there anybody in the same field of business who would benefit from Mr Tansey's death?'

'No...no,' Scaife shook his head. 'There are numerous other brokerages of course, but no close rival. I mean the details are in there,' he nodded to the filing cabinet, 'but the vessels themselves are scattered far and wide, in harbours and boatyards, some are incomplete...you know, a chap sets out to build his own boat, gets halfway through the project and has to give up for some reason or another – we have a few like that. The most northerly on our book is in the Orkneys in Kirkwall Harbour. The most southerly is the quarter of a million pound gin palace in the Mediterranean, which I mentioned. The rest are dotted about the UK with a possible concentration in Yorkshire harbours and marinas, Whitby and Scarborough harbours and Hull marina, because we are local to them, but if you removed them from our books, the majority of boats would still remain. So if you are asking if there is a local rival, then the answer is no.'

'I see. Any dissatisfied customers lately?'

'No,' Scaife shook his head vigorously. 'Benjamin was scrupulously fair with all the customers, both vendors and purchasers. "A good service for a fair price for both sides for a fair commission," that was his motto. It's the logo on the adverts we place in the yachting magazines and it's also on the letterhead of our stationery. So, no dissatisfied customers...no customers at all for the last few weeks. We were getting worried, but we've seen thin times before and always pulled through when the economy picked up.'

'As with most businesses,' Hennessey remarked. 'So you have no idea who might have killed Mr Tansey?'

'None...I do wish I could help you.'

'How did he spend his free time?'

'With his family, I assume. I really don't know, we have little or no contact outside office hours. He has a yacht, it's lying at Hull marina...the *Sea Gypsy*, nice boat, but modest. Twenty-five footer, outboard motor, and he's a member of the Eboracum Sailing Club.'

'Eboracum?' Yellich spoke as if in reflex to Scaife's mention of the name of the sailing club.

'Yes,' Scaife smiled. 'Do you know it? Are you also a member?'

'No...the name, isn't that the Roman name for York?'

'I believe so, except that the "u" in the name is correctly shown as a "v" but to ease pronunciation for the purposes of the club, they have modernised the spelling to "Eboracum". It has no clubhouse; it meets each Wednesday in a room in the Pike and Heron pub in Heslington, midweek, of course, because the members sail at weekends in the summer. It's more social than anything else, has to be because the members' boats are like our customers' boats.'

'Scattered far and wide?' Hennessey suggested.

'Exactly, sailing clubs on the coast can organise regattas and club races, from their bar they can look out onto the water at their boats...but it's fun, we enjoy each other's company. I, too, am a member, though I dare say both myself and Benjamin are members looking for customers rather than members looking for a social life, but one spills into the other.' He wrenched the finger of his left hand. 'Oh yes, one spills into the other.'

'Alright. If I could take your details, Mr Scaife? Just for our records.' He took out his notebook and ballpoint pen. Scaife gave his age as thirty-six and an address in Bishop's Halstead.

Walking down Mad Alice Lane toward Swinegate, Hennessey asked Yellich his impression of Robert Scaife.

'A man with something to hide, I'd say, boss.'

'I'd say so too...the way he pulled his fingers. He didn't like us being there, that's for sure.'

'Didn't, did he? And his address...'

'What about it?'

'I know the village, a lot of nice property there, it's an expensive place to buy in. A lot of small houses...a council estate...but it's regarded as a posh village. Might be a good idea to drive past his address, see what sort of property he owns.'

'Might be.' Hennessey glanced sideways and he and Yellich made eye contact. He glanced at his watch. 'Three pm. No time like the present.' He raised his eyebrows, smiled and Yellich nodded. 'We'll miss the rush hour if we leave now.'

Yellich, as was usual in such circumstances, took the wheel for the drive out to Bishop's Halstead. He parked in the centre of the village besides the fortunately modest war memorial; just seven sons were lost between 1914 and 1918 and two between 1939 and 1945, though a tenth son, one Eric Lee, aged twenty-two, was lost in the Korean conflict in 1952. Nonetheless, Hennessey pondered, it was a lucky village, as villages go.

'Every village raised a stone.' Yellich saw what Hennessey was looking at as he locked the car, leaving one window open by a few inches so as to allow the car to "breathe" in the heat.

'Not true.' Hennessey turned and walked towards the post office as Yellich fell into step with him. 'Not true at all. The war memorials were erected in the 1920s and there grew the myth that every town and city and village and hamlet raised a stone, but in fact twenty-eight did not. I don't know their names...just one of the bits of information I picked up along the way, but they are known as the twenty-eight lucky villages of England. I don't think Scotland, Wales or Ireland has such a claim.'

'Well, well,' Yellich said by means of a response, but he thought it was an interesting fact, the sort of thing that he believed Sara would enjoy hearing.

Hennessey pushed open the door of the post office, causing

the bell to jangle in a soft, welcoming tone. It was pleasant to hear for the first time but he thought he would rapidly tire of it if he had to work behind the counter. It was the sort of noise you'd take home with you and hear in your head as you cooked and ate supper or sat in front of the television. Nonetheless, it was distinctly preferable to the large post office in the centre of York where the employees had to press a button when they were free, which activated a metallic voice that announced their particular window number, so that standing in the queue, Hennessey listened to "window number three"…"window number one"…"window number seven". At least he was able to escape into the bustle of the street after a few minutes but the luckless employees had to endure that all day, each day, and that really would have been a sound that would be taken home and even, he suspected, on holiday, inside their heads…"window number one"…"window number seven"…"window number two". He shuddered at the thought. It was one of those insights into other people's working conditions that made his job seem bearable after all. This post office though was not at all like that, the post office in Bishop's Halstead was quiet and calm inside. The officers walked on bare floorboards up to the grill, behind which sat a silver-haired lady. The noticeboard above the shelf on the right of the room was full of official notices; the wall on the right was quite bare. A successful post office. Hennessey had once been told that successful post offices can be identified by the amount of other work they do, the less other work, the more successful. The post offices that have expanded into becoming a shop on the other hand were struggling. This post office clearly did nothing but Government business and in these days of closures of rural banks and post offices, it had done well to survive. It was, he thought, probably the only post office for many miles around. He walked up to the green painted grill with Yellich beside and behind him. 'Good afternoon, madam.'

'Afternoon, gentlemen.' The postmistress had a soft voice with a distinct Yorkshire accent. 'How can I help you?'

'Directions, please.'

The woman smiled. 'I should have guessed. I know all my customers, even the ones from the next villages, the only strangers who come in only ever want directions.'

'I see. Well, we are looking for Halstead Common Road.'

'Ah...'

'Some difficulty?'

'Well, Halstead Common Road...this village...the road you seek is really in bits.'

'Bits?'

'Yes...it goes from east to west through the village and as the village expanded it got crisscrossed by other roads...and some houses don't have numbers, just names, and some houses don't even have names but the postman knows which family lives in which house. Like in parts of Ireland...the house has a name only and when you are there you think it's going to be a grand and a fine building because all it has is a name, but it turns out to be an ordinary, three bedroom house, just like all the others on the same street. The postman just knows who lives where, you see.'

'I see. Well, it has a name.' Hennessey was impressed by the postmistress's efficient and clearly well rehearsed method of enquiring as to the business of strangers in Bishop's Halstead.

'It's called,' he consulted his notepad and flicked over the pages, 'it's called...'

'Southgate House.' Yellich helped Hennessey, from memory.

'Ah...Mr Scaife...yes, dreadful business indeed...so young too.'

'Oh?'

'Yes, Mrs Claudia Scaife...she disturbed a burglar, you know.'

Hennessey and Yellich glanced at each other. Hennessey

said, 'Scaife, you know I didn't mention it, but I knew that name had a significance.'

'Rang bells with me too, skipper. I remember the case...it went cold very quickly.'

'You'll be the police, I think.' The postmistress became very alert.

'Probably,' Hennessey replied.

'Then you'll *probably* need to turn left as you leave here, then take the third road on the left and you'll find that Southgate House is the first house on the left after you have turned into Halstead Common Road.'

'All the lefts,' Hennessey replied dryly. 'How can we go wrong?'

The two officers stepped out of the shade and the cool of the post office, into the unrelenting heat of the afternoon. Hennessey said, 'Remind me.'

'It was a mess, skipper...bad time for us. As I recall, Tom Denny was the interested officer.'

'Denny?' Hennessey snorted.

'Yes, it was quite a hot case...then there was the arson attack on that house in Clifton...you'll remember that, petrol through the letterbox of an Asian family. The entire family murdered...eight people...three generations: grandmother, parents, the husband's brother and his girlfriend and three children. Horrible.'

'Yes, as you say, I remember that.'

'Well,' Yellich stepped behind Hennessey so as to form a single file in order to walk past an elderly man who walked with his left hand clenched in a fist behind him at the base of his spine, and his right hand gripping a stout looking walking stick. 'Well,' he continued when he and Hennessey were once again side by side, 'all resources were put on that, people were pulled off cases...including Tom Denny...and the arson investigation took full priority. It was a long investigation because we were looking in the wrong place in the beginning.'

'We assumed it was a racist attack, I recall.'

'That's right, so we spent days, weeks, quizzing all known racists and people convicted of racist crime. All along it was a feud within the Asian community. The perpetrators were Asian youths avenging a question of family honour. They've still to go to trial and one, the ringleader, is still at large...believed to have escaped to Pakistan.'

'Yes...it comes back to me.'

'Anyway, by the time Tom Denny picked up the murder of Claudia Scaife again, the trail was well cold. It did indeed appear that she had disturbed a burglar but there were no prints, nothing, no leads at all, so the case was shelved.'

'Makes Mr Scaife's nervousness this afternoon very interesting, very, very interesting.'

'Does, doesn't it, boss.'

Hennessey and Yellich walked on in silence and found both Halstead Common Road and Southgate House to be clearly labelled and would have been easily found by a simple, "third left, first house on the left" direction, but the silver haired lady behind the grill was the postmistress, and she had, albeit unwittingly, given the officers more directions than she had realised.

Hennessey and Yellich stood on the pavement of Halstead Common Road looking at ivy clad Southgate House. They stood in silence, absorbing the image of the building: Victorian in terms of its age, rambling in terms of its dimensions, generous in terms of the grounds in which it stood, and immaculate in terms of the care clearly lavished upon both the house and the garden.

'I'd get rid of the ivy, if I were him,' Hennessey said quietly. 'Plays havoc with the mortar, sucks it dry. Looks pleasant, all that green, but it eats buildings.' Then he paused and spoke for both he and Yellich. 'Now, tell me, how does a man like

Scaife come to be able to afford a house like that, when his employer lives in modest circumstances in Fairfax Street, York Y01?'

'Lottery winner? Did well at York races or the St Ledger? Frankly, I doubt it.'

'So do I, Yellich, so do I. That small office...business in a down swing...his employer's little house and he comes home to this?'

'It's a bit iffy.' Yellich cast a quick, envious eye over the property; it was a house he would be pleased to own.

'Well, let's see if anyone is at home.' Hennessey walked up the drive, Yellich followed, their feet crunching on the gravel. The trees in the grounds cast a welcoming shade. Birdsong. A small animal rustled in the shrubs beside them, as if startled by their sudden presence. Hennessey rang the doorbell, causing a dog within the house to bark loudly, aggressively.

'And this house was burgled?' Yellich turned to Hennessey. 'I mean the gravel...and that dog is no Pekinese... Alsatian...Doberman?'

'Something like that.' Hennessey listened to the bark. It was strong, it was deep, it was defensive.

There was no answer to his ringing of the bell, the dog's prolonged barking did not cause the door to be opened by a housekeeper or similar. There was, in short, no one at home.

Hennessey and Yellich walked round the left-hand side of the house to the rear of the property. They noticed that the garage, which appeared to be a single garage, was, in fact, deep enough to accommodate two cars end to end and with space left over. There was a conservatory built onto the rear of the house into which a healthy-looking Alsatian appeared. It raised itself up by placing its front paws on a metal chair and seemed to look at Hennessey with a mixture of curiosity and alarm. He thought it not to be a particularly aggressive beast; it did not once snarl, for example, and he was impressed by the shiny nature of its coat and a look of warmth in its eyes. It was, he thought, a very well treated pedigree dog.

The garden beyond the conservatory was a wide flat lawn marked out with white lines for badminton or tennis. A garden shed, which, like the house, was evidently well maintained, being painted in green with cream trim, stood in the bottom right-hand corner of the lawn. All was encompassed by trees. It was not hidden from any outside view, but equally, it could not be easily overlooked.

'Reminds me of Sheringham,' Yellich muttered, thinking aloud, 'on a smaller scale, but that same...that same...I don't know...I can't articulate...not smug...'

'Pride?' Hennessey suggested.

'Yes...that's it, skipper...that's exactly it...that's the word I was looking for. This house has a pride about it; Sheringham was the same. I mean, it wants for nothing in terms of upkeep. I imagine it's going to be the same inside, as Sheringham was...neat and clean, inside and out.'

'Doubtless we'll soon find out. I think I'd like to chat to nervous, finger-wrenching Mr Scaife again. You know, Yellich, this house speaks of more than just capital outlay...it speaks of having the money to employ people. Like Mrs Tansey and Sheringham, this garden is professionally maintained, probably not by a live-in gardener, but someone employed, and I'll bet there will be a cleaning lady or contract cleaners.' He pondered. 'What shift is Tom Denny on this week? Do you know?'

'Two 'til ten, boss. He'll be there now.'

'It was very neat.' Tom Denny sat back in his chair. His shirtsleeves were rolled up, an assortment of pens, ballpoints and pencils protruded from an old coffee mug from which the handle had been broken. His desktop was in an untidy state. His manner was relaxed, possibly, in Hennessey's view, a little

too relaxed. He was not an officer Hennessey would have relished working with. Denny's office was in the top corner of
the Micklegate Bar complex, a small room he was obliged to
share with two other "kiddie cops". Hennessey was in no
doubt of the importance and good work done by the child
protection officers, but there was no escaping the fact that
within police culture, 'kiddie cops' do not enjoy the kudos,
the prestige, the honest to God street cred that is enjoyed by
the murder squad, the vice squad, the serious crime squad and
others of that ilk. Denny was in his mid-forties, still at
Detective Constable rank, sidelined, coasting to the earliest
possible retirement, and so it seemed to George Hennessey,
content to let cases cool, if he could, rather than worrying
away at them. Hennessey viewed Denny as the sort of man
who wouldn't see there was work to be done unless his nose
was pushed into it. He had worked with Denny on earlier
occasions, and it was he who had advised Chief
Superintendent Sharkey that a sideways move into the child
protection squad might be in the overall interest of the functioning of Micklegate Bar Police Station. Denny knew of
Hennessey's recommendation and there existed a chill
between the two men.

'The file is in the void.' Denny looked at Yellich, avoiding
looking at Hennessey, except intermittently. He tended to
look at Hennessey when Hennessey asked a question, continued to look at Hennessey when commencing his reply, but
rapidly shifted his gaze to Yellich for the delivery of the bulk
of his reply.

Throughout the meeting, Hennessey contained his anger
at Denny's attitude. The man wasn't going anywhere, he
posed no threat now and would pose no threat in the future.
Hennessey was, however, capable of sensing a feeling of waste
about Denny. Despite his dislike, he saw a man who could
have progressed much further in the police force – if his atti-

tude had been less cavalier, if he had more fully absorbed the protestant work ethic, then...perhaps... 'Neat?' Hennessey asked. 'What do you mean by "neat"?

'Tidy.' Denny shrugged his shoulders. 'Too tidy, too neat, nothing disturbed yet there were indications that the burglar had been in the house for some time.'

'What indications?'

'Well...this was something that the scene of crime officer observed...the weather on the day in question changed...it rained...a sudden downpour which dampened the flowerbed at the point of entry. Footprints in the soil were noted leading away from the house but none leading to the house.'

'So the intruder broke in before it started to rain?'

'Yes, that's what we thought. And left after it had stopped.'

'After it had stopped?'

'Yes, there was no rainwater in the footprints. Now, as I recall...doubtless you'll be going to the file...'

'Doubtless we will,' Hennessey replied, allowing a note of dryness to enter his voice.

'Well, as I recall, we were able to pinpoint the time it started to rain, a lot of folk were caught out in it, so suddenly did it rain and so heavily, that people committed the time to memory. It was just one of those things, they remembered where they were when it started to rain.'

'I understand...I have done the same once or twice.'

'So we knew when it started to rain and we knew when it stopped. Again, it stopped suddenly, it was like a shower being turned on and then, after about an hour or so, it was turned off again. That sort of thing happens in the tropics, I believe...not in the UK. Not often anyway. We phoned the RAF Meteorological Station and they confirmed the times the rain started and stopped.'

'Yes.'

'Now, from memory, the rain fell at approximately

2.00pm.'

'By which time the intruder was presumed to be in the house?'

'That's what we assumed…and it stopped at about 4.00pm. The times are recorded as precisely as we can make them.'

'Okay.'

'Now…Mrs Scaife. Claudia Scaife was seen by a reliable witness at 3.30pm. She was returning to her house. The witness…the postmistress in the village…'

'Yes, we met her.' Hennessey rested his hand on his knee. 'She does seem to know what's going on alright.'

'Gave me the impression of being reliable. She was able to pin down the time that Claudia Scaife called at the post office to within a few minutes. She recalled that they had a chat about the rain. Mrs Scaife couldn't get a parking place near the post office that afternoon, some obstruction…localised road works I think. I mean, it would still be close enough for me and you but madam didn't want to get her hair anymore wet than was necessary. It was clearly bad enough that she had to dash through the rain for the few seconds that it took her to run from her car to the post office and she was not keen to dash back through the rain after buying her stamp or postal order or whatever it was she went to the post office for. Anyway, she and the postmistress commented on the rain and Mrs Scaife pondered whether to wait in the post office to see if it lifted and then said, "It looks as though it's set for the day" or something, and took her leave and dashed back into the rain. Anyway, the postmistress commented that if she had stayed for another few minutes, she wouldn't have had to run back through the rain.'

'The shower was turned off?'

'Yes. Now the distance between the post office and the Scaife house…'

'Is very short…yes, we walked it this morning.'

'Okay. So if Mrs Scaife went directly home, and we assume she did, she was probably turning the key in the front door lock within sixty seconds of leaving the post office…probably a little longer, but within two minutes.'

'Yes, I can see that.'

'Anyway, she was iced immediately after she got home. She was still in the raincoat when she was found and she was found in the front hallway. It's a heavy, solid front door, as you will have noticed, no glass, not even opaque glass or stained glass. So the inside of the hall cannot be seen from outside the house.'

'Yes…the door is still the same.'

'She was hit from behind by ye blunt object…a number of times.'

'A number of times?'

'Yes, someone was making sure alright.'

'Burglars don't murder householders…not often.'

'Not often…but they do, George.'

'Chief Inspector, if you don't mind.'

Denny inclined an upturned palm towards him in a gesture of apology and deference. 'But they do murder householders…not often, still less so with premeditation, but a burglar who panics if a householder returns, can launch into a frenzied attack against said householder.'

'But this seems premeditated.'

'Hard to say…and if he wanted her dead rather than immobilised sufficiently to enable him to escape, it was probably because she got a good look at him and he knew she'd be able to pick him out of an identity parade, or because they were already known to each other.'

'Yes that, or he thought murder was a risk worth taking in order to escape a conviction for burglary.'

'Well, as we find out all too often in our line of work…er…Chief Inspector…there are people out there who

seem incapable of thinking along logical or ethical lines.'
Denny smiled smugly. He was a heavy jowled, thickset man,
with a penchant for shiny gold rings, and a watch, also shiny,
also gold.

'You didn't suspect anyone other than a burglar?'

'Of course…look at the in-laws before you look at the outlaws…I know the rules. We suspected her husband initially
because of the neatness.'

'Again, what do you mean by "neatness"?'

'The house was neat and clean and tidy; it didn't look like
it had been burgled, yet the burglar had been in the house
since before it started to rain and left after it stopped. Mrs
Scaife returned about the time it stopped and was murdered
before she had taken off her coat, so the burglar had been in
the house for comfortably over an hour. It was someone who
wore gloves, plenty of prints of gloved hands in the house,
plenty of time to remove anything he cared to remove and
make good his escape. The implication was that someone was
waiting for her, yet it was someone who had to force a downstairs window to get into the house. It was definitely forced
from the outside. Anyway, we quizzed Robert Scaife, her husband. He was nervous…my heavens he was nervous, kept
pulling at his fingers.'

'Yes, we've also met him. He still has that nervous afflic-
tion. It might mean he's very guilty…it might mean nothing
at all. Unsafe to read anything into it.'

'Yes, it's not what you'd call evidence.' Denny paused. 'He
was not short of motive, stood to inherit a lot of money. The
house was heavily mortgaged with Mrs Scaife being the main
breadwinner. She owned a string of boutiques around the
country. He was employed in a yacht brokerage…a sort of
under manager.'

'He still is.'

'Ah…well, what they had in common was a love of small

boats and she respected him because he was a better sailor than she was and apparently that level of respect was enough to keep their marriage viable, despite the fact that she was earning three or four times more than he was. They also had their finances tied together, they had willed everything each had to the other…which was a substantial amount in her case and a far lesser amount in his. They both had life insurance policies that were sufficient to pay off the mortgage, so both would be financially safe if the other died.'

'Where have I heard that recently?' Hennessey appealed to Yellich. 'Simple repayment coupled with a life insurance policy?'

'Mrs Tansey…or Cross as she insists she is called.'

'Ah, yes.'

'Hardly unusual,' Denny said. 'I have the same arrangement, a simple repayment mortgage with a life insurance policy which will pay off the house if I croak so my family will at least have a roof over their heads…better than an endowment mortgage…don't like those. They're too complicated to earn my trust. Anyway, upon her death, her husband received the life insurance policy payout and paid off the house. Southgate it's called…I think.'

'It is.'

'And he also inherited the string of shops which he sold as a going concern…nice bit of money, I should think…and he also inherited whatever money she had in any bank account she held other than their joint account.'

'No evidence to charge him?'

'None. He didn't really have an alibi, which of course makes things easy for us if we can break it…if it's false that is.'

'Yes, first rule in any felon's book…don't provide an alibi.'

'Well, he did actually, but we couldn't break it. He said he was in Doncaster at the time and that also at the time he phoned home on his mobile phone but rang off when the answering machine cut in. He wanted to speak to his wife, he said, not the machine.'

'You checked that?'

'Yes, as far as we could. In the first place, Doncaster has more CCTV coverage than any town in the UK and we checked the footage covering the route he claimed to have taken through the town and yes, his car was clearly seen at a number of points.'

'But not the driver?'

'Exactly...that issue wasn't lost on us. And yes, his mobile phone was used to phone his house. We dialled 1471 and the last call was from his mobile, but because he didn't leave a message on the answerphone, it could have been an accomplice making the call. And the location of the mobile phone when a call is made can be determined; the signal bounces off receiver dishes that are spread all over the UK, sometimes they are disguised to look like fire alarms, but each dish covers a certain area, and the dish which collected the signal covers an area of Doncaster, just north of Donny as I recall, where the A1 is. And as he said he phoned whilst driving home...risking a heavy fine...it meant he wasn't stationary when he made the call, and so was less easy to capture on film.'

'Not an easy alibi to break...not brittle enough.'

'Yes, in the event he was either telling the truth, or he wasn't. But he did seem genuinely grief-stricken. Then there was the arson attack on that house in the Asian community, eight victims. Chief Super Sharkey devoted everything we had to that, and by the time we had made arrests there, the murder of Claudia Scaife was getting cold...no more leads...and Robert Scaife was just getting on with his life. I mean, no new high maintenance female on his arm, no high living with the money he must have received from the sale of the chain of shops, he was just a widower with a lowly job and a nice house. He was just a normal bloke, picking up the threads of his life...and the case got colder by the day and now...three years on...well, it's now chilled, well past its sell-by date. So what can we do?'

Probably not a lot, Hennessey thought, when he was once again sitting at his desk. In fairness to Denny, there probably was not a lot more he could have done. He sat back in his chair, the accusing finger still seemed to him to point to Robert Scaife; a break in, but nothing stolen...and Scaife seemed to have done very nicely out of the death of his wife. It was, he thought, exactly as Denny had said, the man was either guilty or he wasn't. But if he was guilty, then he was a very cool customer indeed. Underneath all that finger-pulling, all that eager to please nervousness, he was either in control all the while, or he wasn't. If said finger-pulling, eager to please, nervousness was genuine, then he couldn't conceal his guilt, not a man like that, so reasoned George Hennessey as he turned to glance out of his office window at the walls upon which tourists slid in and out of each other's way. But, he thought, once again focusing on the police mutual calendar which was pinned to the wall opposite his chair, if it wasn't his real personality, then he was playing a very cool game, a very cool game indeed, just sitting in his lacklustre job, not drawing attention to himself, probably waiting until the heat died down and content to wait for not months, but years. Cool indeed.

There was a knock on the frame of his door. He looked up and to his right. A young constable stood there, tall, athletic looking, her blonde hair done up in a tight bun. 'The file you sent for, sir.'

'Ah...' Hennessey smiled at the female officer as she approached and handed him the file on the murder of Claudia Scaife. 'Many thanks. Haven't seen you before?'

'No, sir, Constable Pugh, sir, fresh off the press...just out of the police college.'

'And posted here for your sins?'

'Yes, sir, though I feel rewarded for my sins...this is an

interesting station; city and country...a good patch...a good mix of people. The poorest of the poor in the hostels...the country set out in the Vale and everything in-between. I think I am going to be very happy here.'

'Well,' Hennessey nodded. He liked her attitude, her enthusiasm. 'Glad to have you on board.'

'Yes, sir. Thank you, sir.' PC Pugh turned smartly and walked out of Hennessey's office.

Hennessey opened the file and began to read. It was all as Denny had said, and he had been the senior investigation officer. No prints had been found in the house except that of Robert and Claudia Scaife, but there was evidence of a person who had moved from room to room, wearing gloves...but nothing had been moved...nothing removed, the valuables hadn't been collected in a central point. So a burglar, or was it someone looking for something, something very specific...or was it someone waiting for Mrs Scaife to come home? Of the three possibilities, he thought the third the most likely because both a burglar or person looking for some specific item would have disturbed the house. The post-mortem, he noted, with a sense of warmth, had been conducted by Dr D'Acre and had concluded that the death had been caused by "blunt trauma to the back of the head" and that the deceased had been struck a number of times. Somebody wanted her dead, clearly so. The body had been discovered by Robert Scaife upon his return from Doncaster, who had dialled three nines at 18.45 hours that day and who was recorded as being in a "distraught and incoherent state – seemed genuine, unable to be interviewed". The footprint in the damp soil outside the window was of a size ten shoe. Robert Scaife was a size ten but the imprint didn't match any of his shoes. 'So what?' Hennessey said to himself. 'Wear an old pair of shoes to do the job then chuck 'em away – oldest trick in the book.' He turned the pages. He found nothing at all that could point the accusing finger of suspicion away from Robert Scaife. He looked at the photographs in the envelope attached to the file…all in both colour and black white. The deceased, an elegant looking woman in her early thirties, long, dark hair, blood-matted, lying in the hallway of her home, face down, still wearing her raincoat, her handbag lying beside her. Not even that and what it might have contained appeared to have interested the murder. The photographs of the house showed as reported and recorded, all rooms in a neat condition, no sign of disturbance or ransacking, or of methodical search, all seemed to offer up no clues, no leads that Denny might have missed, until Hennessey came to the last photograph. When he looked at it his heart missed a beat. The photograph was a colour photograph of the outside of the Scaife household, taken almost as an afterthought, it seemed, by a Scene of Crime officer and clearly taken at the time of the initial response, for it showed many police vehicles and the black, windowless mortuary van parked in the street in front of the house. But it was the car in the drive, which interested Hennessey; it was a Mercedes-Benz. A silver Mercedes-Benz. Just the type and colour of car which had been reported to have been seen on the rural track leading to the ill-tempered Mr Reed and his farmhouse, close to where the headless and handless body of Benjamin Tansey had been found in a stand of gorse. Hennessey exhaled as he looked at the photograph. He recalled, as best he could, the interviews he had conducted with Mrs Cross and her mother-in-law, the formidable Mrs Tansey of Sheringham. Neither woman claimed to know anyone who owned a silver Mercedes-Benz and Mrs Tansey's claim appeared to have been supported by the warm Jamaican, Henry, the pleasant Henry Chambers whom Yellich had clearly liked, it came through in his recordings, and who had never seen a car of that description at Sheringham. Yet Mrs Cross's claim not to know of anyone who owned a silver Mercedes seemed…it seemed somewhat strange to Hennessey that she should not know that her husband's closest employee, and friend, in a company that employed only two people, Robert Scaife and the secretary, did own such a distinctive car. It was, of course, possible, if he worked in Mad Alice Lane as he did, that Scaife would have had to park his car in a nearby car park and as such it would not have been seen should Mrs Cross happen to have called in on her husband at his place of work. Yet…yet…the Tansey/Crosses and the Scaifes must have socialised, they had worked together for years. The claim of Mrs Cross that she knew of no one who owned a silver Mercedes-Benz suddenly chimed a hollow chime in Hennessey's mind. He picked up the phone on his desk and jabbed a four figure internal number.

'Denny,' came the lack lustre reply.

'DCI Hennessey.'

A pause.

'Yes, Chief Inspector?'

'The Claudia Scaife case…'

'Yes, Chief Inspector?'

'I've got the file here now.'

'Yes, Chief Inspector?' Denny's tone was perfunctory, uninterested.

This time Hennessey paused. He fought to prevent Denny's rudeness getting the better of him.

'The car in the driveway of the Scaife household…a silver Merc…was that Robert Scaife's car?'

'Yes, Chief Inspector.'

Hennessey put the phone down. He felt Denny didn't deserve the courtesy of a "thank you", though he regretted terminating the call because something else had occurred to him whilst reading the file. No house-to-house had been done. That, he felt, was a strange and lamentable oversight on Denny's part. If no neighbour had come forward with information, that of course didn't mean that no neighbour had seen anything. He glanced at the clock on his office wall – 17.30 hours. He was indeed lucky to have caught Denny late in the working day and years after the event. The house-to-house, he felt, could safely wait until the morrow, but before leaving for home he ran a check on the silver Merc's number plate, captured in the forensic photo. *Bingo!* Hennessey thought. It was still registered to a Mr Robert Scaife.

George Hennessey drove home to Easingwold, to the far side of the town from York and to his house, which stood on the Thirsk Road. It was a detached four bedroom property, a solid, confident building, with a garden to the front bounded by tall hedges and a larger garden to the rear, also bounded by hedges. A garage stood separate from the house and between them a wire fence served to keep Oscar confined to the rear of the garden during Hennessey's working day. Hennessey got out of his car and warmed to Oscar's excited barking upon recognising his master's car, the door slam, and the turning of the key in the lock of the front door. Inside the house Hennessey was met by the tail-wagging brown mongrel, which jumped up at him, then ran in tight circles by turns. Hennessey picked up the mail from the doormat, carried it through to the kitchen and opened the back door of the house, preceded by Oscar who exited by the dog flap.

It was by then a warm and pleasant early evening and promised to remain warm until late into the night, so warm in fact, that Hennessey wondered if he would be able to stroll into Easingwold for his customary pint of mild and bitter, in his shirtsleeves. He stepped back inside the house, leaving Oscar crisscrossing the lawn with his nose close to the ground and made a pot of tea. He carried a mug of the tea outside and sat on the bench, which stood on the veranda, and, as he allowed the tea to cool, he began to talk softly, quietly, yet quite distinctively.

'Some old case this one, dear heart,' he said, whilst cradling the mug of tea in his hands, one leg extended out in front of him, the other bent back, tucked under the bench on which he sat. 'It's much as I said yesterday, the headless corpse found in the wood. Confess I wouldn't have seen the significance of a cloud of flies above a mass of furze...or gorse, as they say up here...but then I'm a townie. Didn't really get beyond establishing his identity...with no person that can be identified as having a motive to chop him, and chopped he was, as I told you, chopped with passing thoroughness. Then today...well today, there have been developments...re-opened a cold case of Tom Denny's, a lady murdered at home three years ago. Denny assumed she'd disturbed a burglar, no prints, no witnesses...he did concede the house was unusually tidy considering the "burglar" had been in the house for over an hour, but was essentially, in fact, content to leave it at that. Anyway,' he paused and sipped the tea, 'anyway, turns out that the lady concerned...well, she was the wife of the employee of the geezer who had his head lopped off...both murders are connected. Interesting you might think, wheels within wheels. Turns out that upon her death, said employee became quite wealthy but seemed to be happy to carry on selling boats and marine insurance. It's not a big concern, just three people working in a small, one up, one down sort of outfit in Mad Alice Lane. The sort of job you'd think wouldn't be big enough for him once he had come into the sort of money he'd come into. Life insurance which paid off the mortgage of his not insubstantial house, all the money in his wife's accounts and the money he got from selling her chain of trendy clothes shops. I don't know, dear one, it just doesn't seem right somehow. Mind you, I carried on as best I could...he's probably doing the same as a means of coping...carrying on as before, but alone and cherishing his wife's memory. Police work makes you cynical. I am probably doing the gentleman a great injustice…but yet,' he sipped more tea, 'but yet both he and the widow of the man whose head was separated from his body have denied knowing anyone with a silver Mercedes-Benz, that being the type of car reported to have been seen near to where the body was found, significant because it turns out that Mr Scaife, the employee whose wife was purportedly murdered by a burglar, his car…well, that is a silver Mercedes-Benz. Now what do we make of that, me wonders?' We have the Scaife household and the smaller, ironically smaller house of his employer, and the Tansey-Cross household therein. I doubt that the formidable Annabella Tansey in her huge house with its black servants is involved.'

He drained his mug and went inside his house and did so with a reluctance and yet a sense of a promise fulfilled. In his kitchen, preparing a simple but wholesome meal, his thoughts turned, unbidden, but strongly, to Jennifer, their meeting, both guests at the same wedding, both southerners in the grim north…the getting to know each other, the growing closeness, the marriage, their purchase of the house in which George Hennessey still lived. Her dismissal of the rear garden of their house, then just a flat, green sward as large as two tennis courts, end to end, as "we can do better than that". Better than that she did. One evening, whilst heavily pregnant, she sat at the breakfast bar and redesigned the rear garden. The huge lawn, she decreed, would be divided width ways by means of a privet hedge with a gate set in the centre. Beyond the hedge would be not one, but two garden huts, that would need to be carefully maintained by creosote or paint against the biting east wind to which they would be exposed in the winter months. The remainder of the garden, or the "lower lawn" as she had referred to it, would be given over to apple trees, both eating and cooking varieties, save for a stretch of land at the very bottom of the garden which she had named the "going forth", having once come across the term in

Francis Bacon's essay 'Of Gardens'. In the "going forth", the land would lay fallow, never cultivated, given over to wild sedge, and a pond would be dug and pond life introduced. It would not do, she had discovered, to dig a pond and allow it to fill with rainwater and expect pond life to develop. Pond life has to be introduced from an existing pond. It didn't need much, a jug full of pond water from an established pond introduced to a freshly dug pond was all that was necessary, and the culture would grow in the new pond. She had shown the design to George Hennessey who, in turn, had approved it and the plan took its place on their "things to be done" pile.

The following summer Jennifer died. On the thirteenth day of June, when their son, Charles, was just three months old, she had been walking in Easingwold, carrying a shopping bag, when she was seen to collapse, as if she had fainted in the heat. Folk went to her assistance but no pulse could be found and she was pronounced dead on arrival at hospital, or "Condition Black" in ambulance crew speak. Her cause of death was given as Sudden Death Syndrome, SDS for short, and Hennessey had noticed that it happens from time to time, about once every twelve months he would read a small "filler" in a newspaper, perhaps a paragraph, reporting how a young man or woman – for they all seemed to be young adults – would just die, lose their life, suddenly, without any apparent warning or symptom. They would, like Jennifer had been, be walking along the pavement and then suddenly collapse. There was no known cause, and until medical science advanced to the stage where such a cause may be found, all George Hennessey and the many others similarly bereaved could be offered was that their loved one had died of SDS, leaving them wondering how such a thing could be, and also leaving them finding comfort in notions like, "at least she didn't suffer," and other meagre compensations. George Hennessey had continued to live for Jennifer, completing the garden, where her ashes had been scattered, to her design, and she, being in the garden, he knew he would never sell the house. Each evening, rain or shine, he would stand in the garden or on the veranda, telling her of his day, and lately he had told her of a new love in his life, whilst assuring her that his love for her had not at all diminished, and in response he felt a warmth coming from the garden which could not have been explained by the warmth from the sun alone. All an observer would see was a silver-haired, middle-aged man apparently talking to himself.

Hennessey, having eaten, and having fed Oscar, settled down to read from his collection of military history. His preference was not for the lofty general's eye view of a campaign, but firsthand accounts from the viewpoint of the lowly soldier, and that evening he read from the memoirs of a private who had served with the Lancashire Fusiliers at Gallipoli. It was, he found, powerful in its simplicity, the heat, the overflowing latrines, the dysentery, the lack of supplies and grudging, yet page by page growing respect for "Johnny Turk", who was defending his homeland with skill and courage. Later, when he judged the evening cool enough, he took Oscar for their evening walk, one mile out, one mile back, one man and his dog who loved and trusted and understood each other fully. Later still, George Hennessey took his customary solitary stroll into Easingwold for a pint of mild and bitter, or stout if the fancy took him, at the Dove Inn. Just one, before last orders were called.

It was Monday, 23.00 hours.

Chapter Five

Tuesday, 22nd of July, 09.00 – 14.10 hours
in which a venerable old lady offers information and George Hennessey is obliged to consult his senior officer.

'It's just the way it is in this street…this road.' The man who had initially opened his door but a small crack, now held it wide, satisfied that his two unexpected callers were indeed the police officers they claimed to be. 'Don't like calling it a street, it's not in the city. Halstead Common Road, as you see, not only is it called "road" but its leafy tree-lined nature is more befitting to the word "road" than "street".' The man smiled. He was short, rotund, bald-headed save for a band of grey hair that ran from above one ear, round the back of his head and stopped above the other ear. Spectacles dangled from a cord round his neck. He wore a short-sleeved shirt and shorts, and his feet looked, to both Hennessey and Yellich, to be comfortable with leather sandals. 'We keep ourselves to ourselves, don't live in and out of each others' houses, like some people in the city. That's how we like it, rally round if one of us have a problem…like a burglary. We do that. Keep an eye on each others' houses. It seems to fall to me to investigate every burglar alarm that goes off, for about six houses in either direction. After that, I don't know folk. I'm retired, you see. In all day. Indeed.'

'I see. So…' Hennessey half turned as if to indicate the area behind him, 'so, when Mrs Scaife was murdered…then…then I imagine there would have been a lot of "rallying around", as you put it?'

'Oh yes, dreadful business, disturbed an intruder, so I believe…yes indeed.'

'Were you at home on that day?'

'Yes. Remember that day…all quiet, lovely and

quiet...summer time of the year...just like now. What could be more peaceful? A sudden shower of very welcome rain...we could do with similar right now, my garden is thirsty and they are threatening a hosepipe ban. I have been using bath water and water from the washing up. Plants don't like detergents but it's better than nothing.'

'Yes...so you recall that day?'

'Well...recall it, remember it like yesterday, which is a curious thing to say because I don't actually remember yesterday very well at all. Indeed. Yes. A sign of being busy though, not brain degeneration. Took my long looked forward to retirement and I've never been busier...the garden...the golf club committee...never busier, but I was at home that day. The lovely peace of the road was so suddenly shattered, police cars, ambulance sirens and klaxons. I am quite surprised that the police didn't appeal for witnesses. I thought they did but that's only because I watch detective drama on the television. Spent my working life in hospital administration...strange really, took a job as a clerk thinking it would tide me over until I got a proper job and forty years later, I retired as Hospital Secretary in one of the biggest teaching hospitals in the UK. Indeed. No regrets, that's the main thing, not many men can say that when they reach retirement. Worthwhile job and an inflation proof pension at the end of the road.'

'Yes...yes...' Hennessey held up his hand in a successful attempt to stop the householder's flow. 'So there was no house-to-house done? I mean no house-to-house inquiries made at all?'

'None, none at all. As you see, this house is right opposite the Scaife's, it would have been one of the first to be called upon, I would have thought.'

'I would have thought so too...sorry...Mr ..?'

'Mr Young, Nigel Young...indeed...well, not so old, can still dig the garden and play a round of golf. I have the lowest handicap of anyone over fifty-five at the club…not bad.'

'Yes…yes…so, on that day, did you see anything suspicious?'

'I didn't…not I…not little me, indeed, nor did I hear tell of unusual sights or sounds being seen or heard…seen and /or heard…indeed. Yes.'

'So, in your opinion,' Hennessey asked, 'you think it would be pretty fruitless for myself and Mr Yellich to call on your neighbours. I mean, you seem to have your finger on the pulse of this, this road. If there had been something or someone seen, you'd know, would you say?'

Young smiled as if gratified by the observation. 'Well, I would think so…I would think so indeed, but I tell you who would have seen anything if anything was seen.'

'Who?'

'Mrs Mason, elderly lady who lives two doors that way.' Young pointed to his right, 'Strange lady…widow…widowed young in life I believe, but until very recently, and I mean weeks ago…until a few weeks ago she was always to be seen sitting in her front upstairs window…just sitting there like a hawk on a branch of a tree, watching the world go by, well, what little activity the world sends to Halstead Common Road…which is not a great deal, one murder aside. Not a great deal happens in our road and we like it like that, but if anything did happen, Mrs Mason would have seen it.'

'And she was so "perched" as you say on the day that Mrs Scaife was murdered, or at least likely to have been?'

Young nodded, 'Yes…there is the extreme likelihood that she would have been sitting there…indeed. Oh yes, indeed she would.'

'Rather rules Scaife out,' Hennessey murmured as he and Yellich left Nigel Young's house and walked the short distance to Mrs Mason's house.

'Sorry, boss?'

'Well…if the entire road knows that Mrs Mason used to sit perched in her front room window, the upstairs front room…the bedroom, no doubt, then Scaife would have been included in that knowledge. He wouldn't arrive early and let himself in when there was the possibility that Mrs Mason was perched in her eyrie watching all that happened in the road.'

'Wouldn't, would he? Good point. Wasting our time, do you think?'

'Probably, but since we're here…since we are here, Yellich, for the sake of completion if nothing else, we shall call on her.'

Mrs Mason revealed herself to be a frail, elderly lady, grey hair, black dress, heavy black boots which Hennessey felt must have been very uncomfortable in that heat, though the red shawl that was draped around her shoulders indicated that she suffered heat loss. Her hands were curved and fingers bent with arthritis. Her home seemed to both officers to be in a time capsule of life of an earlier period, caught and preserved. Ink wash drawings in heavy wooden frames hung by visible cords on the wall, bell jars contained stuffed birds sitting on imitation tree branches or on rocks surrounded by imitation moss. The furniture was elaborately crafted and solid looking. The floor was covered with an expensive looking but aged and threadbare carpet. The door had been opened by a maid who wore a black skirt, the hem of which was nearer her feet than her knees, the white pinafore was very white and stiffly starched. After checking both the officers' IDs, she asked them to wait in the hall, which both men found to be musty with the smell of mothballs. She had returned and had escorted them to Mrs Mason, who received the officers in the drawing room.

Hennessey and Yellich stood, showing reverence for the aged, but her appearance disappointed them: here, they both thought, was more likely to be the actuality of brain degeneration referred to by Nigel Young. It seemed that this visit was, as Hennessey said, going to be done for the sake of completion and nothing else. *Straight in and straight out on this one*, he thought.

'I didn't see anything that day,' she said after the preliminaries and, as she spoke, she soon revealed herself to be a woman of mental substance, despite her physical frailty. 'Strange, really.'

'Strange?' Hennessey's hope grew.

'Well, yes. I remember the day well, as we all do in this road, and I did like to sit up in my little nest watching the comings and goings. Not in an idle manner; I had letters to write.' She held up her right hand. 'I could still hold a pen in those days. I have pen pals the world over...well, had, can't write anymore. I managed one last letter to each in a dreadful hand telling each I could no longer hold a pen and that this was going to be my last letter to them, some I had been writing to for years, many years...that was difficult.'

'I can imagine.'

'No...I mean emotionally so.'

'Yes, that's what I thought you meant.'

Mrs Mason smiled at Hennessey. 'Well, as well as the letters to write, and I wrote two each day – one in the forenoon and one after luncheon –there was always the *Telegraph* to digest and the crossword to complete, so I did all that. That's how I used to spend my day, doing that and keeping an eye on the road. I'd rather do that than keep two eyes on daytime television. So that's what I did. Any impression you might have been given about me just sitting in my upstairs window and doing nothing but stare out at passers by, is very wide of the mark.'

'I see. Well, good for you, I say.'

'Will you take a seat, gentlemen?'

'Thanks,' Hennessey and Yellich each sat in a deep and very

comfortable armchair.

'You'll take tea?' Mrs Mason asked.

'Really, we don't…'

'Nonsense, I have so few visitors…I insist. I wonder, young man,' she addressed Yellich, 'the bell…could you?' She indicated a small brass hand bell that stood on a table beside the chair in which she sat. 'I have difficulty doing even that these days.'

Yellich stood, picked up the bell and rang it. He sat down.

'Thanks. These days I depend on Melita popping her head round the door just to see if I want anything.' The door opened. The maid stepped into the room.

'Ah, Melita, a tray of tea, please, for our guests and myself.'

'Yes, ma'am.' The maid stepped silently out of the room.

'I could not manage without her. I don't pay her much either. I pay what I can afford to pay but she could get more as a chambermaid in a hotel. Dear me…to think when I was driving like a demon round the hockey field…I never thought I would become so frail, so dependent…and I wore a uniform when we were at war…now look at me.' She held up her hands. 'Oh, my…'

'You said something about it being strange that you were not at your seat in the window when Mrs Scaife was murdered?'

'Well, never before or since. At the time, it didn't seem connected. I lived alone then, I could manage everything…had a dog…all the companionship I needed, and he was there more for his bark in the night, it led to a comforting sleep knowing he was downstairs. A dog is still the best burglar deterrent. He had the rear garden to roam in.'

'Yes,' Hennessey nodded. 'I have the same arrangement at home.'

'Yes…and Nigel Young, my good neighbour, he walked Toby for me, so he got his exercise. Well, the night previous to the murder, something set Toby off barking, then he'd settle...then he'd bark again...all night...things...small stones rattled off my roof...there was someone out there all night.'

'Did you call the police?'

'No...little point if they remained outside. I would have done if I heard a door being forced or glass being broken, but whoever it was remained outside, any —'

The door opened. Melita entered carrying a tray on which stood a brown teapot, a jug of milk, a sugar bowl and three matching cups and saucers. She placed it on the table beside Mrs Mason, pushing the brass bell away to one side as she did so.

'Thank you, Melita.'

Melita withdrew in silence.

'Where was I? Oh, yes...anyway, the next day...it was so strange...the garden shed had been forced and all the tools my husband used...all had been laid out on the lawn, not just scattered, but laid out, neatly in a line.'

'Unsettling.'

'Very. I confess that that, more than the sounds in the night, made me frightened. The way the tools were laid out like that, it seemed to reach right into me. I found myself shaking...really trembling...I let Toby out, and even he seemed timid...very unsure. So I put the tools back and went back in the house and remained downstairs that day. I felt unsafe at the window and for many days afterwards, if I sat at the window, I had a fear of someone creeping up behind me. It was weeks before I felt comfortable in my window seat.'

'Strange, as you say. So that day you were downstairs all day?'

'Yes...all day...and not only downstairs but also at the back of the house, keeping an eye on the rear garden instead of one eye on the road. I was as far from my window seat as I could be when the murder took place. Later – I mean weeks later –

I wondered if that was the intention: to keep me out of my usual place. I wonder. Could you pour, please?'

'Yes.' Hennessey spoke softly but seriously as Yellich stood to pour the tea. 'Confess, I wonder the same.' He paused as Yellich handed Mrs Mason a cup of tea, which she held unsteadily with both hands, and then wondered further as Yellich handed him one. When Yellich had resumed his seat he continued. 'You must have seen quite a lot of the road?'

'Yes.'

'And not just the road but the houses...and dare I say the households in the road?'

'Oh yes,' Mrs Mason managed a smile, 'like the lady two doors down, still young...had two children and then took a lover by whom she had a third – a love child – to cement their relationship. Oh my, such rows! They spilled out into the street in the middle of the day. That sort of thing does not happen in this road...but they made it happen. No actual violence but the venom from her...just not bothered about people listening, screaming such language, standing at the front gate and he was in the doorway, clearly conscious of an audience, and he said, 'I can see you are a bit tetchy, come inside and we'll talk about it.' Mrs Mason chuckled. 'A bit tetchy...I'll say she was a bit tetchy, but they are still together. Clearly that spat is behind them. But yes, I do see things about houses. Well, I did...and yes, I had a grandstand view of the Scaife house.'

'Anything you can tell us?'

'Such as?'

'Well, anything really, even the slightest, innocent-seeming detail can be very relevant...very significant.'

'Well...a childless couple, not blessed, just as I was not blessed. Unlike the couple two doors away who have the three children, I never saw them argue. She worked very long hours...they told me she had a shop. He worked selling boats.

Always left the house after she did, always got home early...much earlier than she did. Brought his work home too...worked at home, complete with secretary.' She sipped the tea.

'His secretary?'

'Oh yes...a young – well, youngish woman – thirties, carrying what I thought was a thin briefcase...two or three times a week, always looked very, very business like. They didn't conduct themselves like a couple, not walking side by side...she behind him, him carrying a bulging briefcase...she that slim case. Tended to ignore each other rather than pay a great deal of attention to each other, and there were no give away signs like bedroom curtains being drawn shut soon after their arrival. So I don't think there was anything untoward about it. He was just bringing his work home...more comfortable than being in the office and Mrs Scaife would have known.'

'You think?'

'Of course,' she took another shaky sip of tea. 'Well, it's difficult enough for a married man to have an affair without his wife suspecting something, even if he is as discreet as discreet could be, so I would imagine...but he could never bring another woman into the marital home without his wife knowing the instant she walks through the front door...you know, when someone has been in your house, there's a presence. The other woman's perfume will still be in the air and there is no way the marital bed could be used for a clandestine encounter...no matter how carefully you remake it afterwards. I can imagine a man not knowing, but a woman...her home...My late husband had many lovely, wonderful qualities but his head was so full of this and that, that he barely noticed the world in front of his face...it used to annoy me. I wish I hadn't let it annoy me now because we were not together very long – less than ten years – but I would say, "Honestly, you'd trip over York Minster and still not notice it," and once I said that I could drive a herd of cows through this house and he wouldn't see or hear anything. But a woman…her house…of course she'd know another woman had been in her house in her absence and because of that, I saw no reason to suspect infidelity when Robert Scaife brought his secretary home on occasions. Then, just to confirm it, one summer, the summer before Mrs Scaife was murdered – it was a particularly hot day, baking hot, a heat haze was rising off the road surface and the concrete driveways, every window that could open in my house and all the houses I could see, were open – they came home and went into the house and he set up a table and a chair on their front lawn…not the back, as you might have thought, but the front. Then she came out with her slim briefcase and wearing a swimsuit…with her body glistening with suntan lotion. Mind you, that might explain why they put the table in the front garden, the privet was high enough to hide her from view from the road and neighbouring gardens, but from where I was sitting, I could see her. The rear garden would be in the shade you see, especially near the house, so yes, it might make sense after all that she was in the front, getting a suntan while she worked. There's commonsense in that, killing two birds with one stone. Well, she sat at the table and opened up her thin briefcase and started tapping away. It was a portable type-writer you see, a very thin one, but I never saw her put paper in it…but tap away she did.'

'A laptop.'

'A what?'

'A laptop…a sort of computer.'

'Oh,' Mrs Mason sniffed, 'I know nothing of those things, nor do I know anything of those fearful mobile phones. My gardener has one, so does Melita. I wonder…could you take my cup?'

Yellich stood and took Mrs Mason's empty cup and placed

it on the tray, likewise his own and Hennessey's.

'Well, once I saw her tapping away on her typewriter thing, well...well, that confirmed that she was his secretary. Went back to seven down or writing to my pal in Canada or whatever I was doing at the time.'

'I see.' Hennessey sat back in the armchair, once more relishing the high armrests, the comfort of the cushion. 'Now, allowing for the fact that all indications were that there was nothing improper going on between Mr Scaife and his secretary, did you ever actually see the secretary at the house when Mrs Scaife was also present?'

Mrs Mason paused. Hennessey felt that she was struggling for an answer. 'Not that I'd to swear in court.'

'But?'

'But one day, late afternoon one winter, when it was dark about 4.00pm...around the solstice, I watched as a car pulled up outside their house, a man and a woman got out, well wrapped up against the cold; hats, scarves, and carried Christmas gifts up to the house. They were welcomed in and stayed for about an hour, then left, walked back to the car and drove away. I felt I had seen the woman before...couldn't place her, for days, I couldn't place her...but her height, her walk...people have distinctive walks, if you observe long enough, you'll notice that. Then it came to me...'

'The secretary?'

'Well, possibly, as sure as I am prepared to be without having to swear to it.'

'Could you describe the...the lady whom you assumed was Mr Scaife's secretary?'

'Well, short, short of stature, a little over five feet I'd say, don't know what that is in metric, hair black, jet black, about shoulder length. She wore it parted down the centre, wore spectacles when she worked but not when she was walking...needed them for close work.'

'Yes, that's interesting…and the man who brought gifts to the Scaife house just before Christmas one year, what did he look like, can you recall?

'Tall…a good six feet, towered above her, that's all I could see.'

'Do you recall the car the visitors drove?'

'A small black one. Nothing like Mr Scaife's Mercedes nor his wife's Mercedes either.'

'They both drove Mercedes-Benz?'

'Yes. Hers was blue. His was silver.'

Taking their leave of Mrs Mason with words of well-wishing and thanks, Hennessey and Yellich stepped out of the shade of her house into the heat of the noonday sun. They walked side by side down the gravel path that led from Mrs Mason's front door to the road, with Hennessey screwing on his panama hat as they did so. They reached the road and Hennessey turned to Yellich and said, 'Well, well, well…'

'Well, well, well, indeed, skipper.' Yellich held eye contact with Hennessey. 'Short woman, black centre-parted hair, spectacles for close work…there were spectacles on the pile of magazines in Sandra Cross's living room…female spectacles…I mean, spectacles for…'

'Yes,' Hennessey chuckled, 'I know what you mean. I noticed them as well. So, Sandra Cross has some explaining to do, me thinks.'

'It certainly sounds like her.' Yellich looked up and down Halstead Common Road. 'Not unlike the country, is it?'

'What do you mean?'

'Well, these streets, self-satisfied, middle-class suburbia, hardly see anyone but not much goes unnoticed. Like in the country, you can look around you and see nothing but fields, yet you don't know how many eyes are on you.'

'So I believe…so I have heard tell.'

'Well, do we call on other houses? Who knows what has

been seen by whom? I mean since we are here…'

'Your enthusiasm does you credit. We'll split up. Take one side of the road each. If anybody says they did see something, take a note of the house number and we'll call back together. You stay with this side of the road; I'll take the other. We'll meet at the pub.'

'Where's that? What's it called?'

'Don't know and I don't know,' Hennessey grinned, 'but there'll be one, at least one. Ask at the post office, the lounge bar of whichever pub is nearest to the post office.'

'Very good, boss.'

One hour later, Hennessey and Yellich sat once again within a cool interior. On this occasion it was the welcoming lounge bar of the Chained Bull, being the nearest pub in the village to the post office. Yellich and Hennessey chose a shady corner of the lounge, well away from two old boys who leaned against the bar and who eyed them with a mixture of curiosity and hostility. Having been served soda water with lime, and having carried the drinks to the table, a young and slender waitress approached them and asked to take their order for lunch. Hennessey, feeling the need for fortification, asked for the beef casserole. Yellich contented himself with a baked potato with tuna and a salad garnish.

'Frugal?' Hennessey said as the waitress whisked the menu cards from them, turned on her heels and walked smartly back to the door beside the bar over which a sign said "Staff".

'Hot meal on a day like this, boss, don't know how you can manage.'

'I like my food, Yellich, helps me think. Can't really think unless contented.' He looked about him. The Chained Bull seemed to him to be a pleasant roadhouse of a pub. A rural sounding name for a rural pub…quiet, low oaken beams…a pub that seemed to depend on local, rather than passing trade, and which provided the locals with what they wanted; a quiet place to drink beer from the wood. No "smooth flow" beers designed for speedy service in the Bull. That seemed to be clear to him. There was a smell of air freshener mixed with wood polish, real plants on the window ledges, and highly polished brass artillery shells from the Great War behind the bar. Hennessey's own grandfather had picked up some such from the Somme as had many "Tommies" who brought them home in their kitbags as souvenirs to be used in many working-class homes as umbrella stands or ornaments that increased in both sentimental and monetary value. Now, in the early twenty-first century, such artillery shells are, as was Hennessey's experience and observation, only of monetary value – although of considerable and growing monetary value.

'So,' Hennessey turned from reading the pub and addressed Yellich, 'no one from my side of the road saw anything, and no one from your side of the road saw anything.'

'That's the long and the short of it, boss.'

'So, we are left with Mrs Mason's observation. What did you make of her?'

'As a witness or as a person in her own right?'

'Both.'

'A credible witness and a charming old lady, I thought.'

'Yes. I thought the maid...what was her name? Melita. I thought she showed a certain devotion. Mrs Mason is the sort of lady that could command such devotion, unlike Mrs Tansey of Sheringham.'

'Oh yes, totally different kettle of fish, totally different altogether.'

'So where now, Yellich, where now?'

'Well, it depends on which murder we are investigating, boss. Following one murder investigation, we seem to have picked up the trail of another. You'd better clear it with Chief Superintendent Sharkey.'

'Yes, I'll ask for it to be opened to me and cross-referenced to the inquiry into the murder of Benjamin Tansey. His wife is liasing with his employee, wife of said employee is murdered in circumstances suspicious...then he, too, is murdered.'

'Yes, the whole affair has a certain...a certain aroma.'

'Very calm though, just carrying on as normal, Robert Scaife, I mean...Sandra Cross too, if she was party to the murder of Claudia Scaife.'

'Yes, very collected, just ride out the storm of suspicion, carry on as normal. And the display of secretarial work being done in the front garden...quite unusual.' Yellich flipped a beer mat with his fingers and caught it with his hand as it spun in the air above the table. 'Unless it was to put any suspicion out of Mrs Mason's mind.'

'That has to be the reason. It was, as you said, a display. High hedge or no high hedge, what young woman would sit in her swimwear in the front garden tapping away on a laptop? It had to be a performance for Mrs Mason, especially since it was only once...once was sufficient, once was all that was needed. And the clever manner in which Mrs Mason was kept out of the way on the day of the murder; put her in a state of fear, on her guard...a lot of premeditation there.'

The waitress returned with their meals on a tray. Hennessey and Yellich leaned back as the food was set before them, which they received with thanks.

'Mrs Mason has a point though.' Yellich sliced his baked potato, steam rose from it, pleasantly so. 'I mean, Mrs Scaife would have known if another woman had been in her house...certainly our Sara would. I couldn't sneak another woman into our house without Sara knowing, I wouldn't want to but even if I did, I'd never get away with it.'

'That is a point.' Hennessey forked beef into his mouth. 'It's a good point. What do we know about her...Claudia Scaife?'

'Not a great deal, skipper. She must have had family though.'

'You see, that's what I was thinking…a parent who may still be with us, a brother, a sister. Check with the file, will you? Pay a call this afternoon while I am with the Chief Super.'

Again he remembered the boy. The boy he had found in the cupboard under the stairs when he had investigated the scratching and whimpering sounds. He had opened the door and had seen the boy hunched up between the vacuum cleaner and the wall. They had looked at each other, briefly, before he closed the door again. It was, he thought, clearly one more strange happening that he knew nothing of. Like going out to wash the car and finding that it had been done for him; like getting ready to go shopping only to find that some kind soul had already filled his larder and fridge with good, wholesome food. Who had washed his car he didn't know, nor did he know who it was that ensured he had food in his house…and now, now he did not know who had brought a little boy into his house and locked him in the cupboard under the stairs. All he could do was take care of the boy while he was here. He made a mug of warm broth and took it to him.

George Hennessey sat in front of Chief Superintendent Sharkey's desk and once again found himself not envying the people with whom he lived; his wife and children. The Super was, short for a police officer, always neatly turned out, a dark suit with a tie tied into a small knot – far too small for Hennessey's taste, who subscribed wholly to the observation that only small-minded men tie their ties with small knots. His desk was similarly neat; everything in its place, ballpoint pens in a row beside the blotting pad, not needed in the twenty-first century but without which no desk seems to look complete. Behind him there were two photographs in solid frames, attached to the wall. One showed Sharkey in the uniform of an officer in the British Army, the other showed him in the uniform of an officer in the Royal Hong Kong Police, as was. He was ten years younger than Hennessey, but nonetheless very senior in rank. Sharkey listened patiently and attentively while Hennessey appraised him of the progress made in the Benjamin Tansey inquiry, and unhesitatingly approved of the dormant case of the murder of Claudia Scaife being re-opened and allocated to Hennessey. 'A probable link, as you say, George. Can't separate them.' Then, as Hennessey rose, hoping to escape back to his own desk, Sharkey enquired, 'Family alright, George?'

'Yes, thank you, sir.'

'Just the one son, I know, but that's family.'

'Yes, sir, and a daughter-in-law and two lovely grandchildren. Charles is doing well, seems to be anyway, though lawyers always seem to be in debt despite the houses they live in and the cars they drive...fees are a long time coming you see, sir. I don't mean they are poor financial managers.'

'I see.'

'Barristers tend to be prestige customers for banks, who have come to know how the bar works. Barristers are heavily in debt until they are in their forties, then they take silk and start commanding the big fees or are made judges and the word "overdraft" is removed from their lexicon. I think Charles has quite an overdraft but also a lot of money is owed to him for work done. Anyway he seems to survive, keeps cracking the joke about me arresting them and him getting them off, though sometimes he can persuade a felon to see sense and plead guilty –the only thing he can do in the face of overwhelming evidence – though some will still insist on going NG as if convincing themselves they are innocent.'

'Yes, I know that attitude all too well. He is just a criminal lawyer, then?'

'No...not at all, in fact this week he's for the plaintiff in a civil action involving a man who was employed by a firm that provides safety cover on the North Sea oil rigs. A worker fell into the sea, the safety boat was launched, got close to the worker and one man dived in to attempt a rescue…both sadly drowned.'

'Oh, dear.'

'Yes, indeed. Anyway, Charles is for the widow of the man who drowned attempting to rescue the first man, in a compensation claim. The defence is that no claim can be made because the company instructs its employees that they must not leave the rescue craft under any circumstances, that the craft must be manoeuvred close to any person in difficulty and said person then hauled inboard…but Charles's argument is that the company's instructions ignore the human instinct to rescue, and the pressure on individuals to effect a rescue when they are employed in that lifesaving capacity.'

'Interesting…both sides have a strong case, it would seem to me.'

'Yes. Charles told me the company's defence wasn't what he called a "complete defence": it doesn't allow for pressure of the moment or, as I said, human instinct. He is hopeful he will be able to get something for the lady.'

'Well, I'm glad to hear that. He's a bright boy, your Charles. A credit to you.'

'Thank you, sir.'

'Families are everything, George.' Sharkey reclined in what Hennessey thought to be an uncharacteristically relaxed attitude. 'I have two children, as you know, a boy and a girl…well, man and woman now…both at university…Huddersfield and Portsmouth respectively…and both want to join the police.'

'The sense of pride…' Hennessey smiled. 'Yes a family is everything. They ask a lot of a man, but also give a lot in return.'

'Yes…' Sharkey nodded in agreement. 'A family gives purpose to a man's life.'

'Quite. Well, if that's all, sir, I had better get on.'

'Certainly. Let me know how things progress.'

And with that Hennessey turned and left Sharkey's neat – he thought over neat – office, to resume his reading of the Claudia Scaife file.

It was 2.10 pm.

The man screwed the battery terminal down, watched by the little boy, fascinated by the workings of the engine of a motor-car.

'I know what it's like,' the man spoke softly, 'losing your parents when you are young.'

'Do you?' the boy's face faltered. Again the man saw the boy to be lost, frightened...vulnerable.

'Yes,' he said. 'Yes I do...leaves you all alone...'

The boy nodded.

'We could become friends...' the man suggested, 'you and I... Would you like that? Go for a trip in the car...?' He held eye contact with the boy, watching as his face lit up.

'One day,' the man said. 'Soon...' He lowered the bonnet lid and secured it in the closed position. 'Soon, I promise.'

Chapter Six

Tuesday, 28th of July, 14.00 – 21.10 hours
*in which a will is queried, a stranger visits Sheringham, a
suspect is quizzed and a nightmare unfolds.*

'She had no sense of smell.' Diana Townsend sat in a small,
uncomfortable looking chair pushed almost apologetically
into the corner of the small sitting room in a small house on
the Tang Hall estate. Low rise council accommodation, small
gardens, narrow streets, which could somehow manage to
accommodate bus routes, where motorcycles are chained to
lampposts with massive chains held with equally massive pad-
locks. 'It was just her. Just how she was. We didn't have a lot
of money growing up. I still don't now, but it was useful – our
Claudia not being able to smell – because she slept with our
grandmother…Grandma Waite, not Grandma Preston. I still
don't have much now.' She smiled and shrugged her shoulders. 'My man's in prison and he'll not be out for a likely time.
Knew you were coppers…moment I saw you.'

'Your sister?' Yellich held his hand up to stop Diana
Townsend's rambling. He declined her offer of a seat, it was
just one of those houses: a fire grate that had become a receptacle for anything that could be burned – cigarette packets for
the most part, he noted; a carpet that stuck to the soles of his
shoes; a pungent smell about the house, which he thought
Mrs Townsend would probably not notice. Three flies buzzed
against the window, which would doubtless be allowed to
remain until they found one of the open windows in the full-
ness of time. By which time, equally doubtlessly, they would
have been replaced by other flies. Mrs Townsend herself was
portly and appeared not to have washed for a while. She further appeared to Yellich to have probably slept in her clothing.

'Sorry,' she shrugged her shoulders. 'Our Claudia, well she

slept with grandmother Waite…or grandma Waite, who hadn't any control, you know, down there.' She nodded to her lap. 'She wet the bed, couldn't help it. She wore, like, adult nappies, sort of plastic trousers so the bedding didn't get soaked but the smell, couldn't stop the smell…but she and our Claudia liked sleeping with each other and Claudia, not being able to smell…well, it worked out for the family 'cos we were all piled into this terraced house in Holgate, so space wasn't easy to find.'

'No sense of smell,' Yellich repeated.

'Yes. Some people are born blind, some are born mute, our Claudia never had a sense of smell. She did well for herself. Me, I married a rat. My troubles started twelve years ago when I married a rat. Well, he'll not be out for a while: fifteen years for armed robbery.'

'Recently?'

'Last year…be at least ten before he's out. I feel like a schoolgirl at the beginning of the summer holiday.'

'Don't remember that case…'

'Down south it was, Bedford Crown Court. Didn't make the papers up here.'

'What took him down there?'

'The team he was with…very heavy…they hurt a security guard bad, really bad. Nearly got done for attempted murder, he did. Can't keep telling the neighbours he's on holiday, so they know I'm a con's wife now.' Again, a resigned shrug of the shoulders. 'Don't blame you for not wanting to sit down by the way, can't remember when I had a visitor who sat down. You couldn't lend me a few quid? Don't get the social till Thursday and I'm spent up already. I'll let you have it back, 'course I will.'

'Possibly.' Yellich spoke softly. 'It's the old, old story, Mrs Townsend, you help me, I'll help you. You scratch my back, I'll scratch yours.'

'So what do you want to go digging round about Claudia for? You got the animal that did her?'

'Possibly.'

'You didn't seem too interested when it happened. What was that guy's name? Dean...Davy...Denny...that was it, Denny. He said, "He'll surface". Didn't bother chasing after him, doing an investigation. Our Claudia was battered to death and you'd think we'd lost a ball or a pen or something, the "it'll turn up" attitude he had, means you don't bother searching for it. "Just wait and he'll surface," he said. Like Claudia didn't matter. I mean our Claudia, she'd done so well for herself. That big house in the country, a Mercedes-Benz...got a ride in it once when his nibs wasn't there.'

'His nibs?'

'Robert, her husband, he was in Hull one day, selling a boat or whatever it was he did, and Claudia had a day to herself. She drove into York and came out to fetch me and we had tea at a teashop. Later she took me for a spin. Left it parked in the car park, wouldn't bring it onto the estate. She was a bit wary of the lads, and ladettes...ladettes, they're worse, the girls are worse. Claudia, she never forgot her roots, never forgot her family did Claudia, but his nibs...looked down his nose at me, but he wasn't better than us. He came from the streets, no posh background, despite the way he carried himself like he was somebody...and you know the best thing?'

'What?' Yellich replied, knowing he was going to hear "the best thing" anyway.

'Well, the best thing was that that big house was all bought by her, and his car too; all her money. Robert was a clerk, he was nothing compared to our Claudia. He knew when he was onto a winner alright. She could have done much better for herself. Mind you, I could have done as well, but she had more than me, she had looks that I never had. Folk wouldn't believe we were sisters, "There's Claudia," they'd say, "and with her little fat friend," me being the little fat friend. Then she had her money, her a school-leaver at sixteen with no qualifications and worth a million pounds before she was thirty-five! All her own graft, her own hard work. She didn't marry into money, she made it, from a stall in the open market in York, selling ladies' underclothes, to a string of boutiques, selling ladies' gear...I mean, really saucy stuff.' Diana Townsend giggled. Yellich thought that the prospect of ten years without her "rat" had clearly appealed to her. He had the impression of a great weight having been lifted from her shoulders. 'Really saucy...she had shops everywhere, but she never forgot her family.'

'What do you know about her murder?'

'Just what the police told us...surprised an intruder, they said, skull smashed...nothing else. Police...' yet again, a shrug of the shoulders, 'police didn't seem interested. I mean, our Claudia, a successful businesswoman, murdered in her own home and all they could say was "He'll surface". Well, he probably will, but we, our family, would have liked to see a bit more...effort. I mean, if that was the reaction to our Claudia being murdered, I pity the family of a poor street girl, the police would probably say it was her fault.'

Yellich felt uncomfortable. She had a point, she had solid ground for a complaint. 'Well,' he struggled, 'I can't say anything. Mr Denny is a colleague of mine, but what I can say is I...I and my boss, we are not Mr Denny, and I was sent here by my boss to seek what information you can give us about your sister's murder.'

Diana Townsend looked up at Yellich. She saw a tall, youthful looking CID officer. 'Thanks,' she said smiling, 'thank you. I appreciate that, I really do. How can I help you? I'll do it for Claudia, not for any money you can lend me.'

'Well, we'll see about the money, but let's both work for Claudia.'

'Yes. She was too soon in the clay. Lovely girl, the way her eyes would sparkle. I was so proud she was my sister, still am proud, not because of what she did but because, even despite that, she was special. You know yon special person in the world, you meet them from time to time.'

'Yes,' Yellich smiled in agreement. 'I know exactly what you mean. I know very well what you mean.' He paused. 'So, let's not talk about what you know, tell me what you think about the murder. Tell me if there's something, anything, that doesn't seem to add up and deliver.'

'Suspicious, you mean?' She sat back in the small chair.

'If you like. Do you have any?'

'Well, now you're asking…'

'I am.'

'Aye.' She swept her hair back off her shoulder. A futile gesture, thought Yellich, for it fell instantly back into the same place. 'Well, what can I say? Our Claudia…I've never met anyone more observant than she was, if anything was out of place, she'd notice it, so she would. We had a friend once, Big Tony, and it was a long time before we noticed he hadn't got any eyelashes, bit like Claudia being born without a sense of smell. But as soon as Claudia met him, she noticed straightaway and she wasn't close to him. Sure you won't sit down?'

'Yes, thanks.'

'Don't blame you. Mind you, you must see the inside of some houses. Anyway, our Claudia noticed Big Tony's eyelashes, well, you know, straightaway, and she was at the far side of the room. So I can't see our Claudia coming home and not noticing that someone was in the house…she'd know. If she didn't notice anything out of place, she'd sense someone in the house, sense of smell or no sense of smell, you'd know if a stranger was in your own home…our Claudia would.'

'I see.'

'So that didn't make sense to us, knowing Claudia as we did.'

'Interesting point. We have received information Mr Scaife would bring a woman home in the afternoons, possibly as a typist.'

'Yes, that was Mrs Tansey, or Cross as the awkward cow insists on calling herself. Me, I didn't care, I mean, what's in a name. Nothing went on there – it would be impossible for Claudia not to know if any hanky panky was going on, you wouldn't need a sense of smell to find that out.'

'I see…it was something we had to explore.'

'It would look suspicious, but they liked working at home, it was more comfortable than their office. I never went to it but Claudia said it was small…in Mad Alice Lane, I think it was.'

'Yes, it was…still is.'

'Anyway, these days they have computers; they can do anything at home that they can do at the office.'

'Okay,' Yellich adjusted his weight from one foot to the other, 'we can forget that then.'

'What?'

'That they were having an affair.'

'I think you can. If Claudia was suspicious, she'd tell me. We were very close as sisters. She's buried in the cemetery at Fulford. It's two buses from here and money's tight, but I go when I can, tell her what's happening, me talking to a stone…and it's not her in there anyway. I can sit here and talk to her just as easily, but I feel I have to go to the cemetery, even if it's only her bones in the ground, I still go there. She's in the afterlife. Sometimes I envy her, this life can be such a dog sometimes, a real bitch, but the way I see it, we're all in the clay soon enough, may as well walk the dog while you can.'

'That's a good attitude.'

'You think so?'

'Yes, it's a positive frame of mind.'

Diana Townsend smiled. 'It's a long time since anyone has said anything kind to me, a really, really long time. Can I get you a cup of tea?'

'No, thanks.'

'Aye, that's probably wise as well, don't sit down in a house like this, don't take a cup of tea. Claudia would sit when she visited…never forgot her family. We came from a home like this, mess and filth everywhere, Claudia moved away from it, me, I just carried on the tradition. Does it smell?'

'Well…it did a little when I came in…now…'

'Yes, that's what happens, after a while you don't notice the smell, and I live here. How do you expect me to notice the smell? That's how people like me survive, you get folk saying to you, "How can you live like this?" and you say, "Like what?" See, you get used to it and after a while you don't notice it, so that's how.'

'I can understand that.'

'Then there was the will…you know about that?'

'Yes, everything to her husband.'

'All to mother,' she smiled and shook her head, 'all to mother…we learned that.'

'You've lost me.'

'Well, our Claudia, she was worth millions when she died.'

'I know.'

'And she was the woman who never forgot her roots. She'd visit me in this…this hole, and our parents still alive and in poverty, my son and daughter, she took a real interest in them and she doesn't leave us a penny…that was not Claudia, not our Claudia at all. She didn't promise us anything, she never let on what was in her will, but it still wasn't Claudia who'd do that.'

'Who drew the will up?'

'She did…and that's not her either: she was always one for using solicitors, she learned that when building up her business. She got burned a few times on the way up accepting verbal agreements, learned fast, so when the will was produced…well, turned out to be one of those forms, what's called a proforma, I think…like a will you complete yourself, you can buy them from any stationer's.'

'What did she write?'

'She didn't, that was another thing, she typed it. It was fairly thick paper but it had been forced into a typewriter and it left all her property to her husband, I mean everything; car, jewellery, house, business, cash in the bank…everything.'

'Did you challenge the will?'

'Well, yes and no. We went to see a solicitor. We went to one that does legal aid because we'd thought he'd be for ordinary folk like us, but he wasn't keen on having us in his office. But he did speak to us, told us that if the signature was genuine and in the absence of any other will, then we didn't have a case and it would be unlikely that we'd get legal aid to dispute a will. That's when he told us the "All to mother" story. A millionaire died, years ago, didn't leave a will as such but wrote on a bit of paper "All to mother", signed it, the signature was genuine, no other will, so it was agreed it was his will and all went to his mother. So, us being poor folk, we had no money to pay lawyers and had to sit back and watch our Claudia's money go to that waster of a husband. And that waster of a cop, that Denny, he didn't think it suspicious…poor people's justice…no such thing.'

'Does sound suspicious.'

'Well, it's the easiest thing in the world for a husband to get an example of his wife's signature…easy peasy, so easy peasy.'

'What about the witnesses? Her signature would have to be witnessed.'

'See, that's why the solicitor said those proformas were

worthless…and dangerous…too easy to forge. Get a will done in a solicitor's office, he and another solicitor will sign as witnesses to your signature. But if you are drawing up a will in your house, who's to say the witness signatures are not forgeries, anyone can write "Joe Brown" or "Mary White". See my point? Follow my meaning?'

'Yes,' Yellich spoke softly, 'very clearly.'

'And if the only folk to object are folk such as we, and once the estate has been sorted as the will said it should be, put a match to it and where's the proof of forged signatures? Where's the proof of forged anything?'

'Did you see the will?'

'Weren't allowed to. Their solicitors, bank managers…all accepted the signature, so all we smelly relatives could do was stand in the street and sing. No wonder my husband did a robbery. Mind you, I'm well shot of him for ten years.' She smiled, 'And what would I do with all that money?'

'What *wouldn't* you do? Do you recall who their solicitor was?'

'Don't.'

'We can probably find out.'

'How?'

'By asking him…asking Scaife.'

'Getting suspicious?'

'A little,' said Yellich. 'Just a mite.'

It was Tuesday, 14.15 hours.

The man viewed the house. He had taken the bus into York and, in the ancient city, he had taken a second bus for another, shorter journey back out into the flat, green pastures of the Vale, expansive beneath a vast blue sky which, on that day, had just a wisp of white cloud and above the cloud, the long ruler-straight vapour trail of a jet airliner travelling westwards from continental Europe to North America. The man alighted from the bus at a stop outside the Black Swan in Cranswick Nether and walked out of the heat into the cool of the pub, where he ordered a chilled soft drink from the middle-aged barmaid. He found he liked the pub. It seemed to him to have escaped the vandalism of modernisation. There was still plenty of darkly stained wood panelling; old photographs in heavy looking frames hung from hooks driven into ancient plaster; the beams were low and solid; real, not plastic flowers, in vases on the windowsills. Here there was no piped music, no gaming machines, no "junk", which had, in his view, destroyed the inner city and suburban pubs. The other patrons included two old boys who shuffled dominoes on the upper surface of a round table, the second surface beneath was clearly reserved for pint glasses of beer.

The man looked discreetly, very discreetly, at the elderly men and observed just how content they seemed to be in each other's company; both equally leaning forward, both equal in their effort and enthusiasm in the shuffling of the dominoes, then both leaning back, studying the dominoes in their hands. It was a lesson, he thought, in the wisdom of accepting the hand one is dealt in life. It was perhaps a lesson he should have taken on board…but…*too late now…too late*, he thought, *much, much too late*. Not too late in terms of time, but rather in terms of the damage done…the action taken…in terms of the demon unleashed, and that once released can never be recalled. Should he have done what he did? He sipped the cooling drink and pondered…perhaps not, perhaps he shouldn't have, but then she shouldn't have either…shouldn't have done what she did. So he reasoned, if he had done something, then he had done it as retaliation. He did not strike the first blow.

A third patron, also elderly, with the leathery, weather-beaten features of a lifelong son of the soil, sat at the end of the bar eyeing the man with open curiosity as, the man thought, he would eye any and every stranger that bowed his head in order to enter through the low doorway of the Black Swan. The man held eye contact with the older man, who stared at him with an unblinking gaze and raised his glass in his direction, swallowed the remainder of his drink and walked out of the pub into the glare and heat of the afternoon sun, listening to and enjoying the birdsong as he did so. He placed the baseball cap over his balding head, turned to his left and strolled calmly, peacefully, out of the village.

The man reached Sheringham within half an hour of leaving Nether Cranswick and, seeing that the wrought iron gates were open, slid close beside one of the massive stone gateposts, each of which had a lion, rendered in stone, atop of it, and stepped into the shrubbery. He viewed the house from his vantage point within the canopy of a rhododendron bush: the fountain in the centre of the lawn rose and fell, though slightly so, the black servant he had seen so often with a battered hat and baggy trousers, wheeled a wheelbarrow towards the house. Other than that, the man could see no movement. He gazed through a gap in the fleshy, green leaves, across the manicured lawn at the splendour of Sheringham. He thought of the woman in the house, not the black woman, doubtless scurrying attentively at her lowly duties, but the other woman, the white one, "white" so called...the older of the two, and he thought of her grief, imagined her grief, and he hoped that she was inconsolable. 'How could you?' he spoke aloud, 'How could you?' But worse is to come, much worse, and he was, he believed, a man of his word. Indeed, just as he had recently walked down Fairfax Street within the walls, and had glanced into a certain house, and had seen therein the occupant of said house, a dark-haired woman, she standing close to the window – their eyes had met, briefly, but they had met and there had been a look across her eyes, a look that said, "I ought to recognise you but..." He had turned his head away and walked on. He knew who she was, and he had thought, *Be worried…your future is bleak, very bleak…through no fault of your own…but bleak, bleak, bleak because first I will take your husband and then…*

And wasn't he a man of his word? Oh, wasn't he just.

He settled to the ground. Enjoying the shade, the conceal-ment offered by the spreading rhododendron and relished the birdsong. He liked birdsong because the birds were not singing for human enjoyment, a pathetic fallacy. Like saying flowers "dance" in the wind, birds are not at all in song; they will make noises of alarm, or of defence of their territory, but sing they do not…not in the way humans think of singing.

That's why he liked the sound birds make.

They defend themselves.

Again the man pulled at his fingers, one by one. He glanced nervously as Hennessey extended his hand and switched on the recording machine, causing the twin spools to spin slowly.

'The time,' Hennessey said, 'is 16.30 hours. The place is interview room two at Micklegate Bar Police Station in the city of York. I am Detective Chief Inspector Hennessey. I am now going to ask the other persons present in the room to identify themselves for the purpose of the tape.'

'Detective Sergeant Yellich.'

'Walter Bain of Bain, Hargreaves and Cartwright, solici-tors, of York.'

'Robert Scaife.' Scaife spoke nervously, continually pulling at his fingers.

'Mr Scaife…' Hennessey leaned forward, hands together, resting on the polished pinewood top of the table in the room. 'You have been brought to the police station to answer ques-tions in respect of your late wife, Claudia Scaife, particularly to answer questions in respect of her death.'

Scaife paled. 'I…I…thought this was about Benjamin?'

'No,' Hennessey spoke softly, but his tone was serious, 'it

is about Claudia Scaife.'

'Oh…' Scaife looked at Walter Bain, a desperate, pleading look and Hennessey thought Scaife was wearing his guilt on his sleeve. He further thought that it made Denny's lacklustre investigation even more unforgivable.

'My client has not been arrested?' Bain was a well set man, late middle-aged, wearing a dark suit which Hennessey felt must have been uncomfortable when out of doors in the weather that currently prevailed.

'No, sir.' Hennessey addressed Bain. 'Mr Scaife is here of his own free will, that has been explained to him.'

'It wasn't explained why I was brought here.' Scaife sounded agitated. 'I thought it was about Benjamin.'

'Benjamin?' Bain asked.

'Benjamin Tansey,' Hennessey explained, 'is a separate inquiry altogether.'

'He was the guy they found…head and hands cut off, it was in the news.'

'Ah…yes,' Bain nodded. 'I see, now, Mr Hennessey, if my client has been brought here on false pretences, that would invalidate anything he might say that might further incriminate him.'

'Your client, Mr Scaife, has not been brought here on false pretences, Mr Bain, he hasn't been brought here on any pretence or pretences at all. He was asked to accompany my sergeant here to answer some questions, which was all that was said. He then asked for a solicitor to be present and your good self was on the solicitors' duty rota as being on duty.'

'And here I am. I see. Here we are…'

'So, I don't have to stay?' Scaife appealed to Bain. 'I can go?'

'You can,' Bain turned towards Scaife. 'I would be inclined to see what the police want first. I will advise you about your answer.'

'But…Claudia's murder was investigated.'

'Up to a point. It's what we call a "cold case"…not closed, just dormant. Nobody was ever charged with her murder…the case went cold.'

'That doesn't mean we stop investigating,' Yellich added. 'If some new information comes to our attention, then the case is re-opened. We have quite a few such cases…anything can cause them to be reactivated; a chance remark, information offered as a plea bargain by a felon who had some peripheral involvement. We don't plea bargain as such, but if information is given, the parole board in prison will hear about it and will take it into account.'

'That sort of information has helped many a convicted person breathe free air much earlier than he could have otherwise hoped for.' Hennessey smiled. 'So, when information comes to light, new information, we re-open cold cases, as we have done in this case and, as Mr Bain has just said, here we are.'

'So what is the new information?'

'We'll come to that.'

'I'd be obliged if you'd come to it now, Mr Hennessey.' Bain fixed Hennessey with a gimlet stare. 'My client's willing co-operation is not to be trifled with.'

'Very well…Mr Scaife, can you please tell me the exact nature of the relationship between you and Mrs Cross? Mrs Cross, being the wife of the late Benjamin Tansey.'

'Cross, wife of Tansey?' Bain asked, again fixing Hennessey with a stare.

'Yes sir, the lady in question, Mrs Sandra Cross of Fairfax Street, chose to retain her maiden name upon marriage to Mr Tansey.'

'Oh…' Bain snorted with disapproval. 'Yes, I have met the like.'

'The children of the union have the surname of Cross-Tansey.'

'I see. Thank you.'

'Do I have to answer that question?' Scaife pulled at his fingers as he appealed to Bain.

'Will the answer incriminate you in any way?' Bain replied without looking at Scaife.

'No,' Scaife shrugged.

'Well, if your answer is truthful and I am sure it will be, a businessman of your standing in the community, and if it won't incriminate you then you can only help yourself by answering. In a situation like this, it is best not to draw suspicion upon yourself.'

'Well, alright.' Scaife turned to Hennessey. 'There was no relationship.'

'I see. You were seen, on a number of occasions arriving at your home with a lady who was identified as Mrs Cross.' Hennessey knew he was stretching a point.

'Oh...she did some clerical work for us. I bet you have talked to that old woman who lives opposite...always at her window in those days, she didn't miss anything. Yes, Sandra did some typing for us – still call it typing even though she worked on a laptop – nothing wrong with that. We couldn't get a secretary at the time and we worked from my house because it was more comfortable. We can do anything from my home that we can do from the office in Mad Alice Lane. With the computer, all the details are in the machine's memory. They're amazing things. You know the average laptop that you can buy in the High Street today is more powerful than the computer NASA used in the first moon landing in 1969? Then, they were impressed that they had a computer that could be installed in one room...now it's as thin as a small brief case and as light as a handbag,' Scaife beamed. 'Nothing to hide there. Benjy...er...that's Mr Tansey, her husband, knew all about it. He didn't object. He saw the sense of it, he was on the road...travelling. He travelled a lot then, building up the customer base.'

'I see. What about your wife?'

'What about her?'

'Well, did she know? Did she approve?'

Scaife remained silent. He looked at Hennessey as if searching for an answer. 'Yes,' he stammered. 'Yes.'

'Yes? Very big minded of her.'

'She was generous minded.'

'I see...our informant...'

'That nosey old woman.'

'Our informant tells us that Mrs Scaife was never present when Mrs Cross visited your home, for whatever purpose.'

'So?'

'So did your wife ever know when Mrs Cross had visited?'

'Of course, she could tell.'

'Even though Claudia had no sense of smell?'

Scaife looked stunned.

'Smell is the most important sense that a woman would use to determine whether another woman had been in her home in her absence, she would detect the other woman's scent, the other woman's perfume. Very handy having a wife with no sense of smell if nothing is out of place when she comes home.'

'Mr Hennessey!' Bain glared at Hennessey. 'Quite frankly, if you make another cheap insinuation like that, I will advise my client to discontinue his generous co-operation.'

'Very well, I apologise.' Hennessey spoke to Scaife but he noted, with no small interest, how flushed the man looked. It was, he conceded, a cheap insinuation, but the point had been made. Scaife was beginning to look like a man at bay. 'So, changing the subject a little...'

'I'd be pleased if you would,' Scaife snapped.

'But only a little...You mention the elderly lady who still lives across the road from you and who used to sit at her upstairs front window watching the comings and goings below her.'

'Like watching paint dry, if you ask me, not a lot happens in that street.'

'Apart from things like your wife's murder?' Hennessey raised an eyebrow.

Bain drew in his breath noisily, as if to say "careful, Inspector, careful".

'Yes…' Hennessey conceded, but it was clear to him that Scaife, finger-pulling Scaife, under manager of the Yacht and Marine Insurance Brokers, was a very frightened man. He was clearly a man with something to hide, a man clearly shocked to find out that the question of his wife's murder was not, after all – unlike his wife – going to be laid to rest. 'Well, the lady concerned, she told us that something strange happened on the day of your wife's murder.'

'Oh?'

'Yes… She woke that morning to find that her garden had been disturbed in the night.'

'Disturbed?' Scaife continued to pull at his fingers.

'Yes…things…items had been taken from the shed and laid on the lawn…very neatly…not scattered as in an act of vandalism, but laid neatly…very intimidating for her, it shook her to the core, kept her downstairs and at the rear of her house all that day and for a few days after that.'

'I can imagine it would.'

'But, of course, you wouldn't know anything about that, would you?'

'Nope.' Scaife forced a smile. 'No, I wouldn't.'

'It was an effective way of keeping her out of her bedroom window though.'

'Seems so.'

'Useful for you…if…and I say "if" you wished to return home to await your wife and do so without Mrs Mason observing you.'

'Inspector!' Bain snarled. 'Ask my client questions, but don't insinuate, please do not insinuate.' He turned to Scaife. 'Don't respond to that last remark.'

Hennessey paused. 'Very well. So, remind us of where you were when your wife was murdered.'

'In Doncaster.'

'You seem certain...after all these years.'

'It's not that long ago, and yes, I am certain because I remember being asked at the time and it's not the sort of thing you forget. Something significant happens in your life or some significant world event...people remember where they were when their wife said she was pregnant for the first time, remember where they were when they were told their parent was terminally ill...people knew where they were when the Armistice was announced in 1918, or when war was declared in 1939; where they were when Kennedy was assassinated; where they were when they heard about the Twin Towers. Need I go on? And I knew I was in Doncaster on the day my wife...the hour my wife died. Her time of death was fixed to a sixty-minute time window, about which time my car was seen in Doncaster, it was caught on the town's CCTV.'

'Yes. Did you know that Doncaster has more CCTV cameras per square mile than any other town in the UK? That makes it a very useful place for anyone wanting to establish an alibi...just speaking hypothetically now, you understand, not insinuating anything. Want an alibi...drive to Donny...just an hour's drive from York, drive round the town centre a few times and you are bound to be caught on CCTV.'

'Don't respond to that,' Bain growled, as he cast a warning glance towards Hennessey.

'But it's not really an alibi, is it?' Hennessey worried away at Scaife.

'Denny said the same,' Scaife shrugged. 'My car was caught

on CCTV but the driver couldn't be made out...but I made the point that no one else drives my car, he seemed to accept that.'

As he would, thought Hennessey, *as the man would*. Then he said, 'But that doesn't mean exceptions could be made. Did someone else drive your car that day?'

'No.' Scaife spoke in a clear tone.

'Alright. Why did you go to Doncaster that day?'

'To chat to a client.'

'Ah...so you have an alibi. Who was the client?'

'I can't remember his name. It was a wasted journey, he didn't turn up for the meeting.'

'Ah,' Hennessey smiled, 'and that was where?'

'We were going to meet in a pub. He had expressed interest in a boat on our books. We arranged to meet in the pub...I waited for an hour, then returned to York...well, went home...not to the office.'

'I see. I find that strange.'

'What? That I went home, straight home, after a wasted day?'

'No...no...' Hennessey leaned back in his chair, he looked around the room; a pale orange coloured wall from floor to waist height, then pale yellow to the ceiling; a floor covering of brown hardwearing Hessian; a window of thick opaque glass. He turned his attention once again to Scaife. 'No, what I find strange is that you should travel to Doncaster to talk about a boat.'

'It's the way we do business.'

'Really?'

'Yes...really, it makes the whole thing more personal. It helps close the sale.'

'An estate agent would send details of a house to a prospective purchaser by post and answer any questions by phone, but you don't do that?'

'No,' again, a forced smile.

'Where was the rendezvous?'

'A pub. I said so.'

'Which pub?'

'Heavens, I can't remember.'

'It'll be in your diary?'

'Yes, it was, but I discard my diaries at the completion of each year.'

'The company diary too?'

'No...Benjamin insists on keeping them, but I don't necessarily put my appointments in the company diary.'

'How convenient...for your alibi, I mean.'

Bain scowled at Hennessey and then turned to Scaife and advised him not to respond.

Hennessey breathed in through his nose. The scent of air freshener filled his nostrils. 'Tell me, Mr Scaife,' Hennessey once again leaned forward and rested his elbows on the polished surface of the tabletop, 'tell me about your wife's will.'

'Her will? Well, she was fairly strong willed, but she'd listen to reason.'

'Her last will and testament, Mr Scaife.' Hennessey spoke slowly, 'That will, not her personality.'

'Oh, well, fairly straightforward – left it all to me,' he smiled. 'The whole lot; house, business, possessions...everything.'

'You did well.'

'I do not deny it.'

'You sold the chain of boutiques?'

'Yes. Paid off the house with that, put the rest on one side, still had to work...not that wealthy.'

'Really? Is that true?'

'Are you saying that it isn't?' Scaife asked.

'Well, let's just say.'

'No!' Bain snapped. 'Let's not "just say" anything, Chief

Inspector. Ask specific questions, make specific statements, my client is here of his own free will…unless you arrest him.'

'Very well,' Hennessey paused. 'Our information is that you sold the boutiques for a considerable sum of money, more than enough to enable you to give up working for Mr Tansey.'

'Well, your information is incorrect.'

'It can be verified.'

'It can?' Scaife looked worried.

'Easily…the chain of boutiques is still in existence?'

'Well, I presume…'

'If it is, it is a simple matter of asking the present owners how much they paid you for it. This is a murder inquiry and we can obtain a court order to oblige them to release that information.'

'Well, do that then.' Scaife folded his arms.

'You give the impression that you do not want us to know how much you obtained from the sale of the chain of boutiques.'

'I do?'

'Yes, you do. Do you object to us knowing how much you sold the shops for?'

'It's personal.' Scaife shuffled in his chair.

'No, it's not personal, Mr Scaife. It is germane to this very serious murder inquiry. So how much did you sell the shops for?'

Scaife looked at Bain.

'Well?' Bain spoke with an air of calm authority. 'You don't have to answer that, but as the Chief Inspector has said, the information is easily obtained.'

'Two and a half million.' Scaife looked away as he replied.

'And that isn't a lot of money in your eyes?'

'Well…I like working, I have read about those folk whose lives are destroyed by a massive pools win or a massive lotto win. I'd just fill my days with alcohol if I didn't work…drunk at ten o'clock in the morning. Work is healthy.'

'A fair answer, I think, Mr Hennessey,' Bain sniffed.

'Probably,' Hennessey replied. 'It is an answer. Is it the truthful answer, Mr Scaife?'

'Yes.'

'It wouldn't be the case that you were carrying on as normal so as to avoid suspicion falling on you? A sudden selling up of everything and moving to a villa in Spain soon after your wife's death would look too suspicious?'

'Mr Hennessey, please do not insinuate...I must insist.'

'Very well, but you must see things from our perspective, Mr Scaife: suspicion is falling on you.'

'Is it?'

'Yes, frankly it is. Was your marriage happy? Was it a successful union?'

'Very.'

'How long had you been married?'

'Seven years.'

'No children?'

'No, we were waiting. Claudia didn't want to let go the control of her business. She said it wasn't safe to do so, it had to be on a firmer footing before she could take extended time off.'

'Alright.' Hennessey thought it a fair and a reasonable answer. 'Now, turning away from the provisions of the will to the actual document itself.' Hennessey paused as he sensed Scaife stiffen. 'Now, we are puzzled, Mr Scaife...'

'You are?'

'Yes, we are, mightily so. You see...' again Hennessey paused, leaning back in his chair as he did so, 'how to explain this...You see, the impression that is coming across of your late wife is of a shrewd, feet on the ground, businesswoman. Would you say that that is fair?'

'Yes.' Scaife spoke in a guarded manner. 'Yes. She built up her business from scratch.'

'From a stall in the open market, we understand?'

'That's the story, yes.'

'Alright, so a businesswoman, a woman who knows the value of legal contracts?'

'Again, yes...'

'Which brings us to the first puzzle. Why would a woman like that use a will proforma, bought from a shop, which any lawyer will tell you is worth little. I have seen such will proformas for sale and have thought they could only be of interest to someone who either had little to leave in terms of worldly goods, or else was too impoverished to afford a solicitor, or both. Yet, Mrs Scaife had much to leave in terms of worldly goods and would have had a solicitor already engaged to handle her business affairs and further, she had ample means to meet any likely fee for drawing up a will.'

'Is that a question?' Scaife forced a smile.

'I suppose it isn't. I suppose the question is, given Mrs Scaife's means and her clear business acumen, why didn't she have a proper will drawn up?'

'Well...she did. The will you mention is a paper will...in the absence of anything else...'

'Yes, that's the phrase I have heard before...in the absence of anything else, it had to be accepted as her will.'

'I confess, it came as quite a surprise to me.'

'I bet it did,' Hennessey growled.

'What are you implying, Chief Inspector?' Again, Bain jumped to the defence of his client.

'Nothing,' Hennessey sighed. 'I am implying nothing.'

'Good.'

'So, you didn't know that that self prepared will was your wife's last will and testament?'

'I did not. I assumed her will was drawn up by her solicitors.'

'Who were?'

'Firth and Company.'

'They don't do criminal work, do they?'

'No.' Bain spoke with quiet authority. 'Solely commercial. A good firm, expensive, but worth the fees they charge.'

'Are they in York?'

'St Leonard's Place.'

'Should have guessed,' Hennessey smiled.

Bain shared the humour, allowing himself a brief, but distinct smile. 'Well, if you are a self-respecting firm of solicitors and you are in York, you'll want an address in St Leonard's Place, indeed you will.'

'So you knew of your wife's will, but not the content?'

'I knew she had a will,' Scaife replied. 'I didn't know it was one of those do-it-yourself ones, nor did I know the content.'

'Where was it kept?'

'In our bedroom. At the back of a drawer in a large plain brown envelope with "my will" written on it. She kept the envelope sealed, so I couldn't read it.'

'Okay. Any copies?'

'Well, it was destroyed once Claudia's estate had been wrapped up.'

'By "wrapped up", you mean everything she owned was placed in your name?'

'Well, yes, as was her wish. That's the purpose...'

'I know what the purpose of a will is, thank you, Mr Scaife.'

Scaife shrugged his shoulders and fell silent.

'Had Mrs Scaife had her will drawn up by a solicitor, there would have been a copy.'

'I assume so.'

'Yes,' again, Bain offered information, 'the solicitor would keep a copy and a copy is also deposited in a central registry.'

'Is that a legal requirement?'

'Only if a will is drawn up, Chief Inspector. It is not against the law to die intestate and, because of that, it is also not against the law to write your own will. So there is no legal control of the

proformas that can be purchased in newsagents.' Bain paused.
'The self-made wills have caused problems but, by and large,
they are used by those persons whom you have correctly sur-
mised have little to leave anyway, but occasionally a large estate
is divided according to instructions left on a scrap of paper.'

'Yes, Sergeant Yellich has told me, the "All to mother"
story.'

'It's quite famous in civil law and, as you have said, the
phrase "in the absence of anything else" comes into play, as
was the case in the "All to mother" case. No other will, a millionaire's estate all went to his aged mother...wife, children,
they got nothing.'

'I see the importance of having a will drawn up, and by a
solicitor.' Hennessey scratched his chin. 'The other issue that
doesn't ring true for us, Mr Scaife, is the content of the will,
your wife's wishes.'

'She left it all to me. Why is that so curious? I was her husband.'

'Well, the curious thing about it is, that while your wife
made good in life, she apparently never forgot her roots. She
was a regular caller at her sister's house in Tang Hall.'

'Wife of a jailbird,' Scaife smirked.

Hennessey paused. He stared at Scaife. He liked not that
smirk; he liked not the manner of the man who could thus
smirk. 'Your sister-in-law's living conditions and your wife's...'

'Chalk and cheese.'

'Yes, that's the issue, a woman like your wife with her
means, her attitude to her family, would leave something to
them in her will. Her sister would get something, probably
something substantial enough to lift her out of poverty.'

'I suppose she would, but the will just didn't say that.'

'Did her family object?'

'They said a few things, but no legal challenge was mounted.'

'They didn't find a solicitor who would act on a "no win,

no fee" basis?'

'Not as clear cut,' again, Bain offered the benefit of his learning, 'you see, those adverts you might have seen on television don't really tell the full story, they tell a half-truth. The truth that is told is that, yes, if the case fails, the plaintiff's lawyers won't levy a fee, so "no win, no fee", but, and it's a big but, if the case fails, then the plaintiff can be made liable for the cost of defending the case.'

'Ah…' Hennessey groaned, 'I think I see where you are going, Mr Bain.'

'So, raising an action is still not risk free, and this case, I would imagine, hinges on the authenticity of Mrs Scaife's signature?'

'It did.' Scaife spoke with an indignant tone, as if angered that he was no longer the focus of the conversation. 'That's what it did hinge on, the bank manager and the solicitor had samples of Claudia's signature, they both agreed it was authentic.'

'And you had a sample of your wife's signature, I assume?'

'Yes, yes, I did.'

'And was thus in a position to copy it?'

'Mr Hennessey!' Bain glared angrily at Hennessey.

'What did you do, Scaife? Did you trace it, then copy it onto the will proforma?'

'Mr Hennessey, I insist…!'

'Then invent the two witness signatures. Who were they, Mr Smith and Mr Brown?'

Bain turned to Scaife. 'Do not answer that.'

'No intention of doing so, don't worry.' Scaife sneered at Hennessey.

'This interview is terminated,' Hennessey glanced at his watch, 'at 17.33 hours.' He switched off the tape-recorder. 'You are free to go, Mr Scaife. For the time being.'

'For the time being? What does that mean?' Scaife spoke coldly.

'It means what it means, for the time being there's something to dig up here, Mr Scaife, we both know that. I think we'll be chatting again, and chatting again soon.'

'Do not intimidate my client, Mr Hennessey.'

'I'm not intimidating Mr Scaife, Mr Bain. I am merely making an observation. I do, I really do think that Mr Scaife and I will be chatting again, very soon.'

Somerled Yellich drove home to his modest new build house on the Huntingdon estate. As he parked his car at the kerb, the front door of his house opened and his son bounded towards him, threw himself at Yellich, causing him to lose balance at the moment of impact. Yellich put a loving arm around his son and they walked back to the house together, side-by-side. In the house, Yellich found his wife in the kitchen; slender, short hair. She turned and smiled at him as he entered. 'Welcome home, oh Keeper of the Queen's Peace.'

He kissed her. 'So, it's been a good day?'

'Yes,' Sara Yellich smiled at Jeremy, who beamed with pride. 'It's been a very good day.'

Yellich was relieved. Bad days in the Yellich household have been very bad. When Sara couldn't cope with an over demanding Jeremy she had run to neighbours for help and then literally ran away, usually to be found in a quiet part of the old village, in the churchyard, or the meadow by the steam, and had to be coaxed back home with promises of more practical support, more time to herself. It was for the Yellich's, after twelve years of parenthood, still one day at a time. As a reward for being a good boy all day, Yellich took his son for a walk, knowing that Jeremy loved his father's company. They walked to a stream and looked for minnows and sticklebacks and frogs. As a special treat, they walked on, across the fields, across Haxby Road, to the railway embankment where they sat and watched and waved at the drivers of, and the passengers in, the trains, until Yellich senior decided it was time to return home. After the evening meal, Jeremy impressed his father with his newly mastered ability to tie shoelaces and tell "difficult" times like "thirty-three minutes past three".

Somerled and Sara Yellich had experienced the disappointment that all parents experience when informed by an apologetic, fumbling for words doctor, that their son had been born with learning difficulties. Their initial disappointment had, to their surprise, been replaced by a sense of privilege because a whole world, previously unknown to them, had been exposed. They had met the world of "learning difficulties", had met and befriended other parents with similar children, had attended social functions organised by the self-help groups, had listened to talks given by professionals about the nature of the condition, and had been impressed by just what such children can achieve. They had also learned that their son's unbridled warmth and affection, if a little over demanding at times, would never be replaced by surliness, disaffection, rebelliousness and anti-social behaviour when their child reached his teenage years. With love, stability, stimulation, they have been told that by the time he is twenty years old, Jeremy should have achieved a functioning level of a normal twelve-year-old and be capable of supervised, but semi independent living in a hostel. It was something they worked very hard to bring about, and "good days", like that particular day, were very, very welcome.

The woman walked into the police station. She was ashen faced, shaking with worry. She approached the constable at the enquiry desk.

'Can I help you, madam?'

'Yes…I hope so…my little boy is missing. It's gone nine

o'clock and he hasn't come home.'

'I see, madam.' The officer reached for the missing persons form. 'Can I take your name, please?'

'Sandra Cross,' she tried to calm herself, 'number 103 Fairfax Street, York. My little boy is called William.'

Chapter Seven

Wednesday, 29th of July, 09.40 – 18.20 hours
in which a nightmare ends and a man comes to a fork in the road.

'I'm happy to help you all I can, Chief Inspector, but I am obliged to respect the confidentiality of my client's affairs. I will release information of a detailed and confidential nature only upon production of an affidavit with which you can force me to do so.'

'Accepted, sir.' Hennessey smiled. He found Henry Firth to be a warm and welcoming personality, silver-haired, a ready smile, a reassuringly large knot in his tie. His office similarly had a warm quality about it. A large solid desk of dark wood, a maroon coloured carpet, matching embossed wallpaper, and probably, thought Hennessey, probably most interesting of all, was Henry Firth's choice of artwork. It was, in Hennessey's experience, very unusual for a clearly well established solicitor in his late middle years to be possessed of a social conscience, yet the prints on the office wall were of paintings Hennessey understood came from the Realism school of nineteenth-century painting. Not for Firth was the romantic portrayal of rural England. The first painting Hennessey noticed showed a family clearly impoverished, sitting by a roadside under a dark, brooding sky, presumably evicted and now homeless, another painting showed a ploughman slumped over his plough with the horse turning its head as if to recognise a tragedy had occurred; that painting, Hennessey was close enough to read, was called, *The Last Furrow*. Yet a third painting showed two women wearily picking stones from a field, a fourth depicted a queue being formed in the yard of a workhouse. 'Shall we see how far we progress and if we come up against the issue of confidentiality…well, we'll take it from there?'

'Very well,' Firth smiled. 'It's in connection with Mrs Claudia Scaife's last will and testament, I believe?'

'Yes, yes it is. What can you tell me about it?'

'You'll have to be more specific than that, Mr Hennessey.'

'Alright. I understand it was a proforma will?'

'Yes…no secret there.'

'And she left all to her husband?'

'Yes…again, no secret.'

'Did you find that strange?'

'Again, you need to be more specific.'

'It is specific, isn't it?'

'Not at all.' Firth continued to smile, as if enjoying the game. 'It is not unusual for one person to leave all to another.'

Hennessey smiled and nodded his head. 'I understand. What I mean is, did you find it unusual in the case of Mrs Scaife?'

'Mmm…well, this is nudging confidentiality, but I am prepared to answer and say, yes, I did find it very strange.'

'Had she made an earlier will or wills?'

'Wills? Yes, two earlier ones. The first one was significantly more generous to her husband than was the second…about five years separated the two wills…but in each will she made bountiful provision to her family, her sisters and brothers. She had no children, and so, yes, when the final will was produced, which was a homemade…thing…which is an abhorrence to any lawyer…which dictated that all her possessions be left to her husband, yes, it did come as a surprise. The homemade "thing" was dated only a few months after the last of the two wills I drew up for her. She seemed to be moving away from her husband, emotionally speaking, and then, lo and behold, her final will leaves all to him, just a few sentences, "I leave all my possessions, my share of our joint house, all monies in the bank, my business in its entirety, all to my husband Robert

Scaife of…" whatever was their home address…along those lines.'

'Did you suspect foul play?'

'Yes, I did, it just didn't ring true.'

'You didn't raise any concern?'

'No…strictly speaking, once I was satisfied with the signature, I had to arrange the disposal of Mrs Scaife's assets in accordance with her instructions.'

'And you were clearly satisfied with the signature?'

'Yes, it appeared genuine. I have samples of her signature and you could lay the signature on the final will over the samples I have and they would match, perfectly so.'

'It would be the easiest thing in the world for Mr Scaife to forge his wife's signature.'

'Yes, as it would any man or woman their spouse's moniker. If I were to do it, I would trace it rather than try to copy it freehand.'

'Yes…I think I would do that too. I am surprised you didn't voice your suspicions. I feel obliged to say that.'

'Well, I have a duty to my client. I was satisfied with the signature, it was really up to the disaffected parties to raise an action to dispute the will.'

'They live on Government benefit on the Tang Hall estate. They haven't the means to engage a solicitor.'

'They could have reported it to the police. It's a criminal, not a civil matter.'

'They did…the officer was a little uninterested.'

'Ah…'

'So, three years on, do you feel you might have been implicated in a crime?'

'Not in a knowledgeable sense, Mr Hennessey.'

'I wasn't implying that, sir. Shall I rephrase that and say "used" for want of a better word.'

'In the sense of exploited…yes, I think I was. I was sufficiently suspicious to take a copy of it, I did do that. Robert Scaife had to leave it with me so I could authorise its execution. He was, I recall, very anxious to recover it.'

'Well, I think I have grounds to obtain a warrant or a court order to oblige you to let me take possession of the will. We are now reviewing Mrs Scaife's murder.'

'Are you?'

'Yes. The rethinking about the murder was brought about by another case…the headless body found in the country a few days ago.'

'Ah, yes, an intriguing case.'

'Well that person, Benjamin Tansey, was Mr Scaife's employer. The investigation into his death led us to question the original investigation into Mrs Scaife's murder.'

'I see.'

'So, if you could let us have a look at the copy of the will it would save about twenty-four hours of police time.'

'And make me sleep a little easier. I couldn't have prevented Mrs Scaife's death…but…' He reached forward and pressed a bell on his desk. Moments later a conservatively dressed young woman knocked on his door and entered the room. 'Julia, can you obtain the file on Mrs Claudia Scaife, please?'

'Mrs Scaife, Claudia? Yes, Mr Firth.' The woman closed the door behind her as she left the office. Five minutes later George Hennessey was in possession of the names and addresses of the two witnesses to Claudia Scaife's signature on her last will and testament.

It was Wednesday, 10.05 hours.

The woman shrugged her shoulders. She had a smouldering cigarette stuck in the corner of her mouth. Her hair was greasy and matted and hung like a mop around her head. She was, thought Hennessey, in her fifties. She was well built and filled the doorway of the terraced house in Holgate. 'So what?'

'The will of Claudia Scaife?' Hennessey repeated. Children played in the narrow street behind him. To either side washing hung lazily on lines strung out across the street.

'No…will you listen…*his* will, I witnessed his will.'

'Wait…his will? His signature on his will?'

'Aye, that's what I said.'

'Why did he ask you? I mean…'

'Why not? Just wanted a witness to his signature.' Pauline Chapman shrugged her shoulders again. 'That's what I said. He made a joke, unusual for him to make a joke, sour soul that he is, said it means you don't get anything. That's why he gave us fifty quid each.'

'He paid for your signature?'

'Yeah, said it was compensation for not getting anything when he turned his toes up. Fifty pounds, that's a lot of money to me and Molly.'

'Molly?'

'She signed as well.'

'Margaret Carey?'

'Yes, Molly Carey. She lived in the next street.'

'Lived?'

'Aye…lived, poor soul. She's been dead these last two years, never a well woman, cancer. She was only in her forties…just forty-eight, forty-nine, something like.'

'How do you know Robert Scaife?'

'Cleaned for him…office cleaners. Came in and cleaned that little office he worked in in Mad Alice Lane…runs between Swinegate and Petergate. It's a snickelway.'

'Yes, I've been there. Not much to clean.'

'Hardly worth doing it, but we had a few offices to clean, kept us busy from five 'til seven each evening. Came to Mr Scaife's office…sells boats. That little office was about the last we came to. We had keys to let ourselves in but that evening Mr Scaife was there...very unusual, he didn't like working late. You got to know the late workers and those that like to get away early. Mr Scaife was never there. I mean *never* there. We always let ourselves in, Molly and me, did that office last, wet our whistles in the Three Cranes – that's on the other side of Swinegate from Mad Alice Lane – and then went home. A schooner of port each and then home. That night, one summer it was, Mr Scaife was there. Hadn't seen him since he interviewed us before we cleaned for him. Anyway, he produced this will form... the sort you can buy in shops to save you spending money on getting a solicitor to do it for you. Anyway, he had his will all written up and he wanted me and Molly to witness his signature. He explained that that was all we was doing, just witnessing his signature. So we said, "Okay". He signed his name and we signed under it, with our address and the date, then he gave us fifty quid each, said that had helped him a lot and 'cos we weren't getting anything from his will he said he ought to give us something. Can't benefit from a will if you sign it, see?'

'Yes, I see.'

'Anyway, he gave us fifty quid apiece and me and Moll, God rest her, we had more than one schooner of sherry in the Three Cranes that night, we were well out of our skulls. I remember I don't remember going home that night, if you see what I mean...remember I don't remember.'

'Yes,' Hennessey nodded, 'yes, I know exactly what you mean. I would like to get this down in the form of a statement.'

'You want me to come to the police station?' The woman seemed alarmed. 'I don't like police stations.'

'No, that won't be necessary, if you'll allow me to come in, we can do it in your house, if that's alright, Mrs Chapman, but it has to be done. Can't do it in the street,' Hennessey smiled, 'need something to rest the statement form on.' He tapped the thin document case he carried under his arm.

'Aye, come in. Don't want everyone in the street knowing my business.' Hennessey followed Pauline Chapman into her home and emerged some twenty minutes later with a signed statement.

Hennessey and Yellich sat in silence in Hennessey's office.

'Poor woman.' Hennessey sat back in his chair. 'Every parent's nightmare.'

'Aye, solemn…beyond solemn…passing solemn.' Yellich leaned forward, elbows on his knees looking at the floor. 'The collator told me about it this morning, you'd left the office by then otherwise he would have told you, boss.'

'Yes…yes…I'm not upset.'

'He did his checks. Heavens, how much can a human being take, first her husband is murdered…then a week to the day later, her little boy goes missing. She's beside herself. A trained policewoman is with her now. The uniforms are searching every house…the fields. If our Jeremy…I don't think I'd be strong enough…Sara wouldn't.'

But Hennessey wasn't listening, a chill had shot down his spine, his scalp was crawling, he spoke before he knew he was talking. 'There's a link,' he said softly, causing Yellich to look up at him questioningly. 'I wouldn't have seen it but for what you said, "a week to the day", it's too much of a coincidence, Yellich, it's too much of a coincidence. There's a link.'

'There is?' Yellich felt the colour drain from his cheeks; he felt his own scalp tighten. 'There is, isn't there? Don't know what it is, but there's a link. What is it? What on earth is it?'

'Who's in charge of the investigation into William Cross-Tansey's disappearance?'

'DS Last.'

'Better advise him of a possible link to the murder of

Benjamin Tansey…better say probable link.'

'Can I use your phone, boss?'

'Of course.'

Yellich stood and phoned the information for the attention of DS Last. Moments later he resumed his seat. 'So what is it, skipper? Where is the link?'

'Don't know,' Hennessey reached for his Panama hat, 'but I think we bring Robert Scaife esquire back in for questioning. After the statement I took from his cleaner, his ex-cleaner, this morning, he's got some explaining to do about his wife's will.' Hennessey stood. 'Those wills, why didn't he just invent people, fictitious names, an address in bedsit land, we wouldn't have been able to prove anything, we'd be none the wiser?'

Yellich also stood. 'That's often the way of it though, skipper, felons often make our job very easy. But if we focus on Scaife, boss, are we not looking away from the murder of Benjamin Tansey and the abduction of his son?'

'Probably, but he's linked into it at some point, he's in the stew somewhere and right now, he's our only lead.'

'It's better if you don't struggle,' the man looked at the boy, he saw the look of fear in his eyes, 'you can't break that chain.' He paused. 'It's…I'm sorry; it's not your fault. I truly am sorry, but it's not my fault either. You see…you do see, don't you? We are both victims, you and me. It's that cow in the big house…her, your grandmother. It's all her fault. All this, all this is her fault…and your mother…still not buried your father…now…well, I won't say what I was going to say.' He stood up. 'This house is quite remote but don't shout anyway.' He left the room and shut the door behind him. He had a phone call to make.

'It's like a fork in the road,' Hennessey said. 'You can take the easy road or the hard road.'

Scaife looked at Hennessey intently. Hennessey saw that he had the man's attention. He saw, too, that he was worried. He looked pale and drawn. It was often the way of it, Hennessey had noticed; a previous interview that might be inconclusive and after which the interviewee is permitted to leave the station, can have a beneficial effect from a police point of view. The suspect is "softened up" by the process. Middle-class professional people just don't have the hardened attitude of a career criminal; Hennessey had noted that very early in his career. They also have a conscience, which sets them apart from a career criminal and can be made good use of.

'Put it another way, Robert, you can make it hard on yourself or easy on yourself.'

'I knew I shouldn't have done it.'

'What? Shouldn't have done what? Murder your wife?'

'Don't put words into my client's mouth, please.' The youthful looking solicitor, who moments earlier introduced himself for the tape as James Prescott of Lynch & Co., spoke with a solemn tone.

'I didn't say that.' Scaife looked down at the tabletop. 'No, I meant I shouldn't have got the cleaners to sign. There was a little voice in my head saying, "Don't do it, don't do it," but I went ahead and did it anyway. I should have fictionalised the witnesses, found an address of a place where transients live for a few months…real address, but false witnesses?'

'It would have looked mightily suspicious; a woman of your wife's standing and position, getting transients to witness her will. That would have looked very iffy.'

'Yes, but nobody could have proved anything. This way, this way you can prove the will is a forgery.'

'Be careful what you say.' James Prescott raised a cautionary finger. 'Why. That woman, Polly, what's her name…'

'Chapman,' Hennessey reminded him. 'Pauline Chapman,

Polly to her friends.'

'Yes, drunken Polly Chapman…bet she told you she had one after work with her mate, didn't she?'

'Yes. In fact she did.'

'Well, it's not so much a lie as misleading. She had one after work, that's true, but she also had five or six more to go with it. And that was after the five or six she had for lunch. But she kept upright and did a good job, as the other one did, despite having breath like a flamethrower. Maybe that's why I asked them to witness my signature. Perhaps I thought they were so drunk that they wouldn't remember. You know, I bet I was thinking that way. Yes, that was it. I bet it was.'

'How did you transfer the signatures to your wife's will?'

'Tracing paper, then went over the tracing with a pen.'

Hennessey smiled. 'That's how we thought you'd have done it.'

'It was quite easy.'

'So now, now we ask the question…'

'The question?'

'The question…why did you fake your wife's will?'

'To inherit her wealth.'

'Which you have now lost.'

Scaife looked stunned. He turned to James Prescott. 'Is that true?'

'Well, I haven't been engaged to advise you on that issue, Mr Scaife, but yes, it's true, of course it's true. Once a will has been shown to have been fraudulently drawn up, it's null and void. Any of your wife's assets will go to her next of kin. It will go to her father if he's still alive.'

'He is.'

'There were no children of the union? No? Then, yes, it will go to her father. The property of a person who dies intestate goes to parents or children before it goes to siblings. It's like a cross, it goes up or down before it goes side to side.'

'So I'm ruined?'

'Yes,' Hennessey spoke quietly. 'Yes, you are. It also puts you well in the frame for the murder of Claudia Scaife.'

Scaife remained silent.

'You benefited wholly from her will which we now know you forged. Why forge a will unless you intend to benefit from it? You would hardly forge the will if you were going to wait for your wife to die peacefully in her old age, and you would do it about the time of her death, just before or immediately afterwards. Polly Chapman recalls witnessing your signature during the summer months. Your wife was murdered during the summer, three years ago.

'Sandra Cross was a frequent visitor to your house when your wife was absent and, conveniently, your wife had no sense of smell, and the elderly lady, Mrs Mason, who sat at her upstairs window was, on the day your wife was murdered, intimidated into remaining downstairs by something which had not happened before or since. You knew about Mrs Mason in her bedroom perch. You had motivation.'

Scaife turned to Prescott who said, 'Say nothing.'

'So tell us the true nature of the relationship between you and Sandra Cross. Not even the most innocent boy scout would believe that you and she went to your house all those afternoons to do office work, despite doing some work in the front garden once or twice to attempt to deceive the ever watchful Mrs Mason.'

Yellich, sitting next to Hennessey, spoke for the first time since the interview commenced. 'No jury in the world will believe you were not having a romantic liaison. Where did you go? One of the spare bedrooms?'

'The basement…the cellar, actually. We went to the cellar.'

A silence fell in the room. The twin spools of the tape recorder spun slowly, silently, recording what all four men knew was going to be a confession. The silence lasted, so far as Hennessey could estimate, for about thirty seconds. It seemed a long time in such circumstances.

'We built a love nest in the cellar,' Scaife explained. 'You see Claudia, she had another condition that she lived with; she suffered from arachnophobia...she is terrified of spiders...she didn't just scream if she found one in the bath, she would freeze in terror, fixing her eyes on it...she just didn't go into the cellar.'

'Useful for you,' Hennessey observed, then regretted saying it: this was no time for cynicism, no time for sarcasm.

Scaife glanced at Hennessey as if to rebuke him for the remark. 'So we had our liaisons, me and Sandra. The magic had gone from her marriage, the magic had gone from mine.'

'So you murdered your wife, then you murdered her husband.'

'No!' Scaife shouted. 'No...no! No! Neither she nor I had anything at all to do with Benjamin's murder. I mean, banging somebody over the head is one thing, but chopping their head off...' Scaife's voice faltered as he realised what he had said.

'Well,' said Hennessey, quick to pounce, 'that's so near a confession that you couldn't get a razor blade between the gap.'

Scaife paused. He glanced at James Prescott, who avoided eye contact.

'I mean, look at it from our point of view, Mr Scaife: a forged signature on your wife's alleged last will and testament; a will that leaves everything to you from a woman who was concerned about her family; a witness who will state she witnessed your signature on a will, not your wife's; the removal of Mrs Mason from her window on the day of your wife's murder; an admission that you were sleeping with your employer's wife; an admission that the magic had gone from your marriage; you had no money, you lived out of your wife's pocket; no other suspect and now you have said, "Banging someone over the head is one thing". The only person banged over the head in this case was your late wife.'

'It's all circumstantial.'

'Perhaps, but you see, Mr Scaife, there comes a point, not in each case, but in many such cases, that the weight of circumstantial evidence has been sufficient to convict. I think the Crown Prosecution Service would run with this…but there's more.'

'There is?'

'Yes, there is. There is whatever Mrs Cross will tell us. You may not know this…'

'I do.'

'What?'

'That her son is missing. She phoned me last night. I went over to Fairfax Street but the police were there, I felt in the way. He's still missing?'

'Yes. She is reported to be beside herself with worry, as you can imagine. It wouldn't be appropriate for us to question her now, especially about a crime, even a murder that is three years old, but we can wait, even if the outcome of her son's abduction – because after this length of time abduction is what it most likely is – even if the outcome is a tragedy, at some point we will be speaking to her and a mother who has lost her son will not have the resilience to stand up to quizzing. She'll be shot through with guilt. If she assisted in the murder by driving your car where you both knew it would be picked up on CCTV, namely Doncaster, and belt and braced that by making a phone call on your mobile when in the Doncaster area, knowing that call would be logged by time and location, and should she choose to turn Queen's evidence against you, she could negotiate a reduced charge, and a reduced sentence.'

'She could do that?'

'Oh yes, and if she is sensible, she will do that.'

'But it was her idea.' His voice faltered again.

'Can I have a word with my client, please, gentlemen?' Prescott asked without raising his eyes.

'Certainly.' Hennessey reached for the STOP button on the tape recorder. 'The interview is postponed at 15.20 hours in order for Mr Scaife to take legal advice.' He pressed the button. Hennessey and Yellich then left the room.

Annabella Tansey put the phone down softly. She felt physically sick, and had to work hard to keep the contents of her stomach in place. Then she picked up the phone again and dialled 1471. The recorded voice told her that she was called that day at 15.21 hours and gave the number of the phone the caller had used. She wrote the number down on the edge of that morning's copy of the *Daily Telegraph*. She dialled 1471 again to confirm that she had written the number down correctly. Then she dialled 999.

Hennessey and Yellich stood by the automatic vending machine in the corridor outside the interview rooms. The door of interview one opened, James Prescott stood in the corridor and in an expressionless tone of voice said, 'My client wishes to make a statement.'

'He could be out in ten years.' Hennessey placed Robert Scaife's confession in the file of Claudia Scaife's murder.

'You think so, skipper?' Yellich sat in front of Hennessey's desk.

'I think so. Going G to it, as my son would say, genuine remorse, he'll be sentenced to life, of course, but in his case that's going to be nominal, ten years' good behaviour, he's not a career criminal. If he volunteers to clean the toilets and helps the illiterates to learn to read and write, yes, I can see him walking in ten years. Won't have much to come out to. All his money, all his property in the hands of his wife's family, less any he siphoned off, possibly put in a building society we don't know about, but frankly, I don't think he would have done that.'

'Just leaves us with the distraught Mrs Cross to talk with about conspiracy to murder. Can't arrest her at a time like this, surely?'

'Difficult. She'll hear about his arrest, that will finish her, but at some…' Hennessey broke off as his phone rang. He let it ring twice and then answered it. Yellich watched Hennessey's brows furrow as he listened to the phone call. Then Hennessey said, 'Hang on, I'll ask.' He held the mouthpiece away from his head but made no attempt to cover it, the caller was clearly allowed to hear the conversation between Hennessey and Yellich. 'This is Tom Last, DS in charge of the investigation into the abduction of Sandra Cross's young boy.'

'Yes, boss?'

'There's been a development…links to us.'

'We said it would.' Yellich sat forward.

'Mrs Tansey, the elderly lady who lives in that huge house, what's it called? Town in Norfolk.'

'Sheringham.'

'Yes, that's it. She's received a phone call from a man claiming to have her grandson.'

'What did he say?'

'He said, "That'll be the end of your line, won't it?"'

Yellich felt his jaw sag. 'So Scaife didn't murder Benjamin Tansey, his murder was unconnected.'

'Probably. Anyway, the caller didn't shield his number and so Mrs Tansey was able to get a result when she dialled 1471. The call was made from a call box near Sledmere, out that way.'

'That rings bells.'

'And the gardener at Sheringham reported someone loitering in the grounds, hiding in the shrubs as if sighting up

Sheringham. You know gardeners and countrymen; they don't miss anything. The gardener said he reacted as if he hadn't noticed the intruder, but he described the man as middle-aged, balding but with a bit of silver hair, wearing a blue baseball cap, and he seemed to have a little red rucksack beside him. He wonders if that means something to us?'

'It does. What was the name of the fella who found the body of Benjamin Tansey, said he was curious about a swarm of flies hovering over gorse?' But Hennessey was already reaching for the file on the murder of Benjamin Tansey.

'His name is Swannell.' Hennessey spoke into the phone as he read the file. 'Nigel Swannell and he lives in a cottage just off the road between Sledmere and Garton-on-the-Wolds. Rendezvous with you in the car park, now, this instant. We'll take you there.'

'No, no, I wasn't playing games.' To the officers, Swannell looked genuinely puzzled. 'I do things...things like that. I have lived alone for a long time, and I do things I don't remember...like...like coming into the kitchen of a morning and saying, "Oh somebody's cleaned it," then days later, I realise I had cleaned it. Sometimes I remember doing things...sometimes I don't...'

'Do you remember abducting the little boy?' Hennessey asked. Yellich and Last watched Swannell's reaction but remained silent.

'No, I don't... Someone had brought him to my house and I just fed him... But I do remember killing Benjamin – but only after I found his body. If I had remembered killing him, I wouldn't have called the police...that worked against me.'

'Why did you kill him?'

'Revenge, the oldest motive in the book.'

'Why? What had he done to you?'

'Him? Nothing, nothing at all. He was my half-brother.

No, I wanted revenge on that female in the big house.'

'You are her son!'

'Yes…ten years older than Benjamin. I wasn't wanted…she got well rid of me, couldn't make her way in the world with an illegitimate infant…got rid of me…one home after another. I was "difficult to place" because of my personality, foster home placements kept breaking down and I ended my childhood in a children's home. I was in a mental hospital before I was twenty, but managed to hold down a job in a bank. Changed my name by deed poll, just didn't want to be called Semple. I'm an honest man…never stole a penny. So, this is a cell?'

'No,' Hennessey said softly, 'this is an interview room. A cell is a little less comfortable than this.'

'Anyway, a few years ago I began to find things out, accessed my Social Services file…took some time to track her down, married woman called Tansey, it's not a very common name. I tracked her down, found out she was big on the family name, so I thought, *what's the worst thing I can do to her*? Then I realised it was to destroy the thing she had abandoned me to create…so she would die knowing her line was going to die with her.'

'Would you have killed the little boy?'

'Probably, if I remembered that it was me that kidnapped him…otherwise I would have left him for the person that brought him into my house. But if I remembered kidnapping him then, yes, I would have put him with his father's head and hands – they're about a foot down in my shrubbery. His body was too big to bury so I carried it into the gorse where I thought it would rot away without being discovered…but then I forgot I'd done it and saw the flies and thought, *hello, what's attracting them*?'

'How did you lure Benjamin Tansey to your house?'

'Contacted him, explained who I was. We met a few times…gained his trust, eventually he came out to my house for dinner. When his back was turned...bang...I remember doing it now, for a while I didn't.'

'Why cut his head and hands off?'

Swannell   shrugged.   'I   don't   know...a   lot   of reasons...anger. Anger at him, anger at my mother...wanting to damage what she wanted...make it worse for her to have to bury just bits of her other son... Stuff like that...I wasn't thinking straight.'

'And the silver Mercedes you reported parked in the lane?'

'Never was one...but Benjamin's business partner had one...attempting to throw you off my trail.'

'Alright,' Hennessey sighed. 'We'd better get this down in the form of a statement. Are you certain you do not need a lawyer?'

'Certain.'

It was Wednesday, 18.20 hours.

'Well, it's too complicated for me.' Hennessey wiped his hands on the oily rag. 'I also wouldn't want to risk doing any damage, lovely old lady that she is.' He took hold of the bonnet catches and closed the folding bonnet.

'I'll phone the garage, they'll come and collect it.' The woman looked at Hennessey with adoring, dilated eyes. 'The proprietor has made me promise him first refusal if I ever want to sell it, which means he lavishes tender loving care upon it whenever I leave it with him. Won't though, it was my father's first and only car and when the time comes, I'll give it to my son.'

'Aye.' Hennessey patted the bonnet and, still holding the rag, turned to face the woman. Behind her was her impressive half-timbered house, around them was the village of Skelton with its eleventh-century church and ancient yew tree. 'Yes, strange case really. Sandra Cross's relief at the return of her son was followed hard by her despair at having her collar fondled for conspiracy to murder, but I think both she and Robert Scaife will get lenient sentences.'

'For murder? Lenient?'

'Well, he'll get a nominal life term, but he'll be a good bet for early parole. She's capitulating as well, going "guilty" and not offering any defence. For her...I'd say five years, out in three. My son always says it's better to play with a straight bat. If you are guilty, say so, it will be reflected in your sentence. Sandra Cross's son has gone to live with his grandmother in her huge house where, no doubt, he'll be spoiled rotten. As will Scaife's Alsatian; he was taken in by Mrs Mason...just the companion she needs, and he trots between the two houses, guarding both...a very happy animal!'

The woman smiled, still fixing Hennessey with adoring eyes. 'And the man who started it?'

'Nigel Swannell? He seemed to retreat into a world of his own shortly after we took a statement from him…the psychiatrists just couldn't reach him, he was zombie-like. He was admitted to a secure psychiatric facility under the provisions of the Mental Health Act, unfit to plead, totally unfit…he'll be there for many, many years. He'll still be there when Robert Scaife and Sandra Cross are breathing free air again and picking up the pieces of their lives. So do we really have time?'

'Yes,' Louise D'Acre smiled. 'My ex is keeping the children for an additional night, we have the rest of the afternoon, all the evening…all the night, all tomorrow until about five pm. Let's go up, put you in a bath before we do anything else…'

'You can join me,' Hennessey smiled.

'You know,' Louise D'Acre slid her arm in his, 'you know I might just take you up on that offer.'